Swift River Secrets

ALSO BY J.A. McINTOSH

The Meredith, Massachusetts Series

———————

Niagara Fontaine
Judge Hartwell
Grampa Leary

Swift River Secrets

J.A. McINTOSH

Swift River Secrets
Copyright © 2024 J.A. McIntosh

This is a work of fiction. Though the Swift River Valley Historical Society is an actual place, and one that should be visited, all characters and events are the products of the author's imagination. Actual places and organizations are used fictitiously.

Produced and printed by Stillwater River Publications. All rights reserved. Written and produced in the United States of America. This book may not be reproduced or sold in any form without the expressed, written permission of the author and publisher.

Visit our website at
www.StillwaterPress.com
for more information.

First Stillwater River Publications Edition.

ISBN: 978-1-963296-56-3

1 2 3 4 5 6 7 8 9 10
Written by J.A. McIntosh.
Cover photograph taken by J.A. McIntosh.
Cover & interior book design by Matthew St. Jean.
Published by Stillwater River Publications,
West Warwick, RI, USA.

The views and opinions expressed
in this book are solely those of the author
and do not necessarily reflect the views
and opinions of the publisher.

For Mac and Billy Callahan
Curiosity is everything

Bauman Family Tree

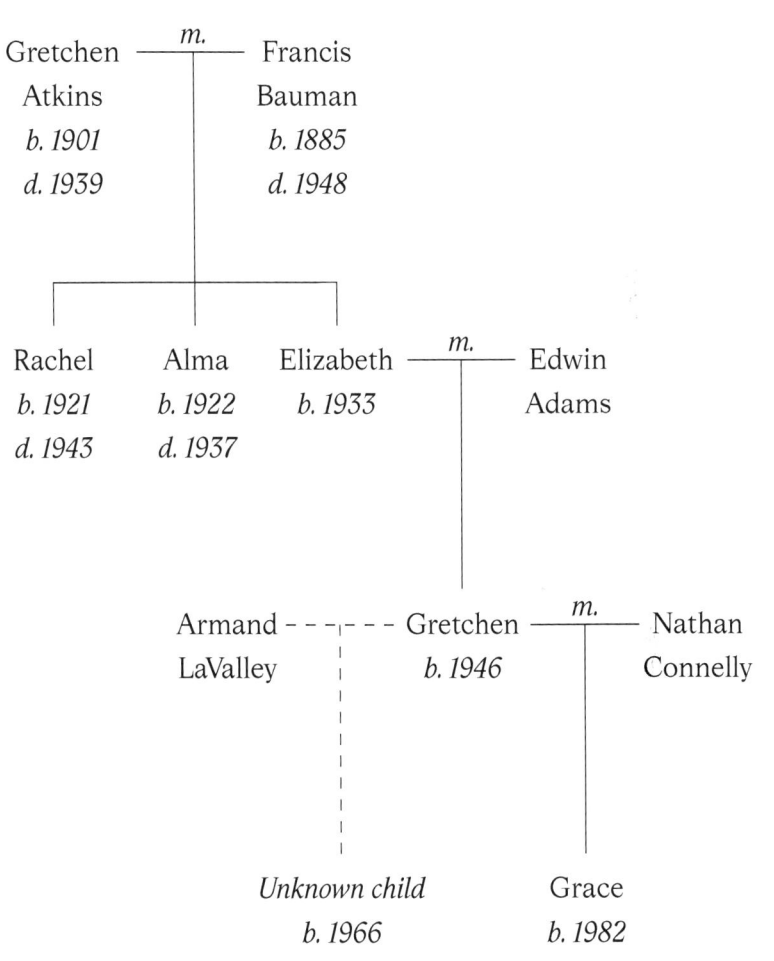

April

CHAPTER ONE

I lost my shoe as soon as I left the cement path. The mud sucked it off my foot and I stood there, on a raw April day, toes red, trying to balance on one foot. I've lived in New England all my life and should know the hazards of mud season by now. But, when I opened my purse to take out my keys, the to-do list I created that morning flew out of my bag and onto the last of the dirty snow. I went to pick it up and ended up shoeless.

Of course, it was my fault for wearing such impractical footwear, but my feet were swollen this morning and these were the first shoes I found that fit. I pulled the silver shoe with the kitten heel out of the mud, took a tissue out of my purse, and smeared the semi-solid dirt all over the outside. Due to years of yoga, I didn't tumble into the mud, despite the awkwardness of my newly pregnant body. I wasn't showing yet, but my pants were too tight. When the inside of the shoe looked clean, I slipped it on and continued on my way. Past the Prescott church, the carriage shed, and to the Whitaker-Clary House. My meeting with Grace at the Swift River Valley Historical Society was scheduled for two and my phone said it was already eight past. It also said that I had twenty-three unread messages.

I wasn't looking forward to the meeting. Some items had gone missing from the historical society, and Grace was the last person to see them. Nothing in the museum was worth over five hundred dollars; we'd had the items professionally appraised just last year. On the other hand, the documents and equipment were irreplaceable. I'd agreed to meet in the unheated farmhouse because Grace had denied the items were not in their usual places. I'd been the archivist here for almost four years. I'd tagged and catalogued and examined everything in the collection. It was highly unlikely I was mistaken.

I clomped toward the large, white farmhouse that served as the primary exhibit for the museum. To this day, it lacks running water and central heating. A fund drive raised half the amount needed to update the house. It did have electricity and I hoped that Grace had already turned off the alarm system. That alarm system and I had ongoing issues.

I went to the back of the house and walked up the short flight of stairs leading to the summer kitchen. The door was unlocked. My shoe was leaving tracks on the stairs so I pulled out the entire packet of tissues, wiped off the shoe again, and debated going next door for water. That would make me later still, so, putting the cold shoe back on my foot, I pulled open the door and went inside.

Except for the alarm panel with its green light blinking across the room, I could have stepped back over a hundred years. The wood cook stove stood to my left with the wood box beside it. Also in the room was a spinning wheel. When I started at the society a few years ago, I took cooking lessons on the wood stove, as well as spinning lessons. I still shudder to think about the burns on my arms and laugh at the tangle of wool through the spinning wheel. I'm an archivist and decided to stick to documents and artifacts.

At the moment, the cold room only hinted at the summer season. Cobwebs hung on the dry sink and the icebox. The cleaners wouldn't show for another month. I started making a list in my head of what needed to be done before we opened. Dusting the artifacts, checking for winter damage, getting damaged items to the restorer, training the incoming docents about their tasks and how to conduct tours, and getting ready for the next board of directors meeting. Irene, the administrative coordinator, would help me, but she'd only been on the job a few weeks. All that would have to wait. I needed to concentrate on Grace and the missing items.

I walked into the main living area, with its huge cooking fireplace. Mouse droppings littered the hearth. Some living things used this as winter quarters. Except for the residue of the mice, it didn't look like there was another living being in the area.

"Grace," I called. "Grace, are you here?"

No answer. I stored my winter purse, waterproof and large enough to contain gloves and a hat, behind the desk, slipped my phone and my keys into my pocket, and looked around the room. Grace's backpack was leaning against the bookcase. Some shades had been opened to let in the sun. I was fanatical about the shades; they had to be closed at the end of every shift so that the sunlight did not damage the vintage exhibits. No footsteps upstairs and, had Grace been up there, she could not move around without the weathered floorboards creaking.

I walked down the hallway toward the front door. As I do every time I enter the Whitaker-Clary House, I went to my favorite exhibit in the museum. It's a watercolor painting by Olive Molt. The museum owns twenty-two of her paintings, but this is my favorite. It shows a house in the Swift River Valley with a spray of flowers off the roof and over the front door. Nobody knows whether this was an actual house in the valley, or a picture that the artist had in her mind of how valley life should be. It's beautiful. When I do tours, I always stop at this painting and tell the story of Olive Molt. She was an art teacher in Chicopee, Massachusetts who married an engineer when the Swift River Valley dam was being built. Shortly after their marriage, she contracted tuberculosis.

Her husband hired a caregiver for her and the caregiver drove her through the valley so that she could paint pictures of the houses that would soon be torn down or shipped away, because her husband's project was going to flood the valley. I imagined this woman, ostracized by her community because she married an engineer seeking to flood the valley, suspected by her husband's coworkers because she lived nearby, and driven to paint by a desire to preserve a way of life fast disappearing.

Something caught my eye off to the left in what was originally the dining room, now the Enfield Room, named after one of the lost towns of the Quabbin. The braided rug on the floor had a dark stain on it. It was a reproduction but a society member had hand-braided it. Fearing some damage done over the winter, I entered the room. No cleaning materials were kept in this building, so I'd have to go next door for supplies. Good, then I could get something to clean off my shoes. First, I needed to determine the extent of the stain and what needed to be done to clean it up.

I followed the brown stain under the center table, and found Grace lying on the floor. She was on her left side, with her arm under her head. Her hair, normally a brassy blond, had the same brown stain, and the Enfield town seal, eight pounds of metal, lay near her head. She was not moving.

I knelt and turned her toward me; her arm fell to the floor with a thud. I felt for a pulse. Nothing. Her skin was cold, but it was chilly in the room. What the hell was going on? I looked around and didn't see anyone else and I would've heard them had they been upstairs. Nobody to help me or Grace. What happened to her? It was unlikely that she'd hit herself with the lead seal, attached to a lever to imprint the town stamp. Who had been here with her? And why leave her in this condition? I felt tears run down my cheeks. For Grace, who was in bad shape, and for me, because I didn't know what I was supposed to do next. Deep breath, assess the situation.

I'd had lifeguard training—archivist jobs were hard to come by—and been trained in CPR. But I needed help. Pulling my mobile phone out of my pocket, I considered calling the New Salem police chief directly. Because of our relationship, I knew he'd drop everything and come immediately. Problem is he's a part-time chief with a full-time job at the house of correction; this requires that he turn off his phone at work. Quickly discarding that idea, I dialed 911. Prayed that I had service, always a problem in this rural area. I put the phone down next to Grace, rolled her onto her back, and started CPR. No need of my own checklist here; the first aid instructor had drilled the essentials every class: A (airway), B (breathing), C (circulation), D (disability), and E (environment). Grace's airway wasn't blocked, but she wasn't breathing; I needed to puff air into her. Circulation would be helped by CPR. Grace didn't have any disabilities and the environment, while cold, was not an issue.

"911, what is your emergency?"

"My friend has been injured. I'm at the Swift River Valley Historical Society, 40 Elm Street, in New Salem, Massachusetts." I was precise because I had no idea where the 911 dispatcher was. She could be forty miles away on a sprawling, interconnected network. Concentrating on the details also meant that I didn't have to think about how awful this could be.

"What's your name? And what town did you say you were in?"

I blew two puffs of air into Grace's lungs, hoping it did some good. Then I answered the dispatcher. "Emma Wetherby. I'm in New Salem. North central Massachusetts." More compressions. This didn't seem to be working. Was I doing this correctly? It had seemed so straightforward in class. But I had to do something; Grace was depending on me.

"Do you need an ambulance?"

"Yes. And the police." Not likely that Grace hit herself over the head.

"I'm notifying the ambulance and contacting the state police. Please stay on the line."

Two more compression cycles. Still no response. I asked, "Are you still there?"

"Right here." Though the voice was distant and professional, I'd have breathed a sigh of relief, had I any breath left.

"Ambulance is on the way." A short pause. "Is her airway blocked? Is she breathing?"

"Not breathing," I said. My shoulders and neck were tight, and I tried to relax them. Even my teeth hurt, and I'd only been at this a few minutes. "I'm doing CPR. Is there something else I should be doing?"

"You should also be doing resuscitation to get air into her lungs. Hang on, I'll check with the ambulance."

"I'm doing the breathing too," I said. "It doesn't seem to be helping."

"I've been in touch with the ambulance personnel. Can you describe the victim?"

"Her name is Grace Connelly. She's in her forties, healthy, fit. She does have mild asthma." She didn't look so fit right now. Her skin was gray. Why wasn't this working? What else should I be doing?

"That's good. You're doing fine. What are her injuries?"

Pain radiated from my knees due to kneeling on the wood floor. Made me forget that my shoulders ached. Where the hell were the EMTs? Why did I have to do this alone?

I pushed on her chest again. Damn, I wish she'd wake up, or gasp, or belch, or something. Even throw up on me.

"She has a head injury. She was hit with a metal object." I tried to keep my voice calm and even, but I wanted to know when help would arrive.

"Is she bleeding?" asked the dispatcher.

"The bleeding seems to have slowed down or stopped." Was that good news or bad news? I had no idea.

"Keep up the CPR," said the dispatcher. "The most important thing is her breathing and her circulation."

I did some more compressions and breaths. It felt like knife blades in my knees and back. Damn it, Grace, wake up.

Silence from the phone. I glanced at it and saw my rescue mutt and screensaver, Barney. The phone was working, so was I, but where was the dispatcher?

"ETA four minutes," said the dispatcher. "How are you doing?"

"I'm getting tired and my shoulders hurt." I don't usually whine, but this was exhausting. Two more rounds. "I think she needs more help than I can give her."

A siren. An ambulance siren, one of the best sounds ever heard. "The ambulance is coming. I hear it." Now that I knew help was near, my brain got foggy and each compression required concentration. "Tell them the back door is open." If I couldn't help Grace, I could get the EMT team in the right place.

"Good, just a few more minutes." The dispatcher sounded like my yoga instructor, urging me to do just a little more. Now this was about to end, I just wanted someone else to make the decisions.

The ambulance crew was noisy; I heard them tramp up into the summer kitchen. Then the Enfield Room closed in when the two attendants, a man and woman, pushed a gurney through the hallway door.

"We'll take it from here," said the man.

My hands were aching and I was grateful I didn't have to keep pressing into Grace's flesh. But these two EMTs looked like they'd just graduated from high school. What the hell did they know? They had a breathing bag and other equipment I couldn't identify and they pushed me out of the way.

I tried to stand and toppled onto my butt. Maybe this pregnant body was more than I could handle.

"Emma, are you still there?"

I picked up my phone from the floor. The dispatcher was still on the line.

"I'm here. The ambulance people just arrived." I heard a noise behind me and turned to look. "And the state troopers too."

"Good. Do you need anything else from me?"

I felt the pain again, radiating from my lower back, up my spine. "No, I'm good."

"I'll hang up now." The dispatcher disconnected.

I stared at my phone on the floor. Tried to figure out what I needed to do next. Move, as I was in the way; there were too many people in the room.

"Do you need help getting up?" This from the female EMT. "My name is Katie and I can help you." She put her arm under mine, and I struggled to my feet.

"I need to call my partner," I said. "Tell him what happened."

My call went directly to voicemail.

"Todd, something awful has happened. I'm fine, but the ambulance and police are at the historical society. Swift River." As if I worked anywhere else. "Please come as soon as you can." I disconnected with the vague feeling I should do more to reach him.

"Are you okay?" Katie looked up into my face.

I nodded. "Why aren't you taking care of Grace?"

"Grace is dead." Katie sounded genuinely sorry. "There was nothing you could've done. She's been dead for a while."

I'd known this was true from the minute I started CPR. But I kept hoping that I was wrong. "But our meeting was scheduled for now." I looked down at my phone. "Twenty-five minutes ago." Tears blurred my vision. Great, brain fog and tears.

"I'm no expert," said Katie. "But her skin is cold."

My skin was cold too. "Why did she come so early to this house? That doesn't make any sense." Grace was dead, that didn't make sense either.

Katie pulled her jacket around her. "It's almost colder here than outside. Come on, let's move out of here." She led me into the hallway.

"There's no central heating in this building. It's only open from June to September." I sounded like the tour guide, probably not helpful right now. As I walked, my head started throbbing and another spasm went up my spine. I put my hands on my lower back.

"Do you need help?" Katie held out her hands.

"My back hurts and I'm dizzy," I said.

"Miss, we need to talk to you." This from a woman in a state trooper uniform. She had black hair and dark skin, in contrast to her male partner with blond hair and freckles.

"I'm Trooper Gray," she said, and waved in the direction of her partner. "And this is Trooper Bachelor. We need to talk to you about what happened here."

"She looks pale." Katie stepped into the doorway and addressed her partner. "I'm going to take care of this lady," she said. "Are you good here?"

"Can't do anything here," said a disembodied voice. "I'll just wait for the medical examiner. Unless you need me."

"No, I've got this." Katie put her arms around my shoulders. "Does your back still hurt?"

No way to avoid telling her. "I'm pregnant," I said. Somehow, making that admission started a cascade of all the feelings I was trying not to acknowledge. Anger at Grace for dying, shame that I'd accused her of taking things, frustration that I had to deal with her death, and an overwhelming feeling of being alone and unprepared. I started bawling.

Katie put her arm around my shoulders and handed me a wad of tissues. "Let me examine her before you question her. Make sure everything's alright."

It took a moment for me to realize she was addressing the troopers. I wiped my eyes, blew my nose, and tried to look like I couldn't answer any questions right now.

She fetched her bag, listened with her stethoscope, and checked my oxygen and blood pressure. Same routine I went through at my prenatal visit.

"How far along are you?" asked Katie.

"About twelve weeks. My clothes are just starting to get tight." I pulled on the elastic waist of the pants, one of the few pairs that still fit me. Much more practical than my kitten-heeled shoes, which were now cold and wet.

"Everything looks good." Katie put everything back into her bag. "Though I'd like to get you out of the cold. Are all the buildings unheated?"

"There's heat in the church, but it's turned down low because nobody's scheduled to be around today. And a bathroom too." I looked around. "I need to stay here, make sure the antiques aren't damaged. I'm responsible for the museum."

"I'll take care of that," said Katie. "You go with the state troopers." Katie went into the Enfield Room. I heard her voice and then that of her partner.

"Let's go." Trooper Gray took my arm. "We need some information. Would you be more comfortable talking in the church building?"

I nodded and we started out the door and down the walk to the church. I knew Katie had other duties, but I wished she could stay with me.

We approached the front entrance of the church, just as another state cruiser pulled into the parking lot on this side of the building. Two more troopers got out of the car. Trooper Bachelor stayed with me while Trooper Gray went to talk to the new arrivals. After a brief conversation, Gray rejoined us on the church steps.

"This how we get in?" asked Gray. "Or is there another entrance?"

"The offices are in this building, and a conference room. A kitchen and the archive room too." I stared at the front door, uncertain what to do next. "It's the only building that's heated." I felt my eyes filling with tears. "I want to call my partner."

"Do we go around to the office doors?" Gray gestured toward the back. "We need to get to the conference room."

"There's a handicap ramp too." I wasn't answering her questions. Grace, lying on the floor; the picture kept popping into my mind. Grace, who loved to be in this church.

"Tell me how we get in." Gray put her hand on my arm. "We can't sit on the stone step."

"I've got a key." I pulled the keys, with the SRVHS lanyard, out of my pocket. "I put them in there when I went into the house. It wasn't locked."

She took the keys from me. "I'll open it." She inserted the key and moved the door back and forth. It stood firm.

"There's a trick to it," I said. Maybe I couldn't do anything about Grace, but I knew how to solve this problem. Taking the key from Gray, I pulled the entire door toward me, and turned the key. With a final push, the heavy wooden door swung inward.

CHAPTER TWO

We entered the Prescott church. The late afternoon sun came through the stained glass windows, highlighting the dust particles in the air. This was a classic New England church; the windows were just squares of colored glass, with the name of the donor inscribed at the bottom. No elaborate panels with Christ praying or the holy family escaping to Egypt. Grace had a special fascination with the stained glass windows; most were paid for and dedicated to a person long dead, and she knew the history of each window and every family. She was always delighted when the family of one of the donors showed up and she could point to a piece of the family history. One more thing Grace will never do again. I took tissues out of my pocket and dabbed the tears from my face.

Nobody went into the church in the winter; it smelled stale and dust covered the exhibits. More mouse droppings in the corner. Some creatures had enjoyed being away from the snowy world. Though it was no longer a functioning church and no services were held there, it was set up with rows of pews. Most were covered by red velvet cushions, an extravagance the original congregation might frown on. I sat and looked around the church. Grace would never see this again.

A clanging, metallic sound filled the air. I put my hands over my ears.

"What is that noise?" asked Bachelor. He looked toward the white panel on the wall, now flashing red. "How do I disarm it?"

I forgot about the alarm. Fumbling for the lanyard, I pulled it out of my pocket.

Bachelor walked to the panel and pushed some buttons. The blaring sound continued to penetrate all corners of the church.

"The code's on the card, with the keys!" I shouted.

Bachelor looked down and then pushed some more buttons.

Blessed silence. For about thirty seconds. *Bang, bang, bang.* The entire wooden front door shook.

"Hey, you guys in there? I can't get the door open."

Gray yanked open the door. Two troopers stood outside. They might have been the two that Gray spoke to before we entered the church, but I wasn't sure.

"Are you alright?" the shorter trooper asked. "What was all that noise?"

"The alarm went off," said Gray. "Emma forgot to mention it was armed."

"It's not my fault," I said. I glanced at the keys, still in Bachelor's hand. "We've got to call the alarm company, or we'll have the police and fire department here." The last time I'd forgotten the alarm, the town threatened to charge the society for the unnecessary call.

"The police are here," said the trooper standing on the steps. "We'll take care of it."

"But you're supposed to call the alarm company." I stood up.

"You look like hell," said the unidentified trooper. "You should sit down."

Bachelor jammed the keys into the hand of the trooper on the steps, with instructions to call the alarm company; the number was printed on the card. "And don't forget to search all of the buildings."

The two troopers on the steps left, leaving me with Bachelor and Gray.

They got me downstairs and through the office area. I excused myself and went to the bathroom where I tried to call Todd again. Still went straight to voicemail. I left a second message. "Todd, the state police are here. As I said before, I'm fine, but please call."

When I emerged, both troopers were sitting in the conference area. I joined them.

"Tell us about the layout of the museum," said Trooper Gray.

"There are four buildings. The Whitaker-Clary House, the carriage house, and the Prescott church. The barn is used for storage only." This was basic information for me, and I was glad the troopers started with something I knew. Maybe that's in the state interview and interrogation manual. I didn't want to think about Grace. But, of course, I did, when I mentioned the main house. "The church sanctuary is how we entered. The lower level has an archive room in the front, with a kitchen and bathroom, and a conference area. There's a cupola too, but only the bats are up there."

Bachelor made a note on a pad he took out of his pocket. "We'll have to search the cupola too."

"Why?" I asked. "Nobody goes up there."

"That makes it a great place to hide," said Gray.

"Hide?" I hadn't considered that whoever attacked Grace might still be on the premises. The idea that I might be in danger never made it to my list. "Why would someone stick around if they'd just committed a crime?"

"Some people like to watch." Bachelor made another note on his pad.

"Do you want or need anything?" This from Gray, guess she's the good cop. "Are you doing okay?"

"There's bottles of water in the kitchen fridge." I waved in the general direction. "I think one would be good right now."

Gray returned and put the water down in front of me. "Morning sickness? Or something we need to worry about?"

"I'm feeling better." I took a drink of water. "I have a scheduled appointment with my ob-gyn tomorrow, but I should be good until then."

"We'll need to check this building." Trooper Gray went to the door of the archive room and tried to turn the knob.

"It's locked." I got up, retrieved the key from the office, and unlocked it.

"Please wait here while we search." The troopers went into the front room.

The troopers returned quickly and I took them upstairs to search the main body of the church. The stairs to the cupola were in bad repair and covered with bat guano and cobwebs. It didn't look like anybody had been up there in years, but the troopers went up to check anyway.

Trooper Gray came back down the stairs, removing cobwebs from her hair. She started talking before she hit the bottom. "We've cleared the church and the trooper securing the scene is searching the house and the other buildings."

Another trooper, one I hadn't seen before, entered the church. "Can I talk to you?" He directed the question to Gray.

Gray told Bachelor to take me downstairs. We left the two troopers with their heads together, talking in low voices.

Trooper Bachelor led me back to the conference room and pulled out a chair for me. "Are you doing okay?" he asked.

"No, I'm not doing okay," I said. "I don't find a dead body every day. It was horrible, all that blood and she wouldn't start breathing. I knew she was dead, but I was hoping the paramedics could revive her." I felt more comfortable dumping on Bachelor, now there was only one trooper. "Let's get started. I want to get this over with. I want to call Todd, my partner, again. Last time I called, he wasn't answering."

"We're not going to discuss the specifics of what happened," said Trooper Bachelor. "Not until my partner finishes upstairs and joins us. You can call Todd when we finish."

"How long will that take?" I heard myself whining. I'd kept it together this long, I could hold out for a few more minutes.

"She's just giving out assignments, it shouldn't be long," said Bachelor, "but I don't want you to have to say everything twice, so we'll wait for her."

"I'm not sure I can sit here in silence." I knew the trooper was lying. I would be telling my story several times before this was over. Maybe he was obeying the chain of command. Or there could be a more sinister reason why both troopers had to be present. I'd found the body and I'd accused Grace of taking things. Maybe I needed a lawyer. At Trooper Bachelor's suggestion, I got a piece of paper and started taking notes on what I remembered. I hadn't filled half a page when Trooper Gray returned, carrying a black case with a wide bottom, made to stand up on its own.

Gray sat down next to Bachelor, across the table from me. She put the file case on the floor, took out a recorder, and put it on the table. "Okay, tell me what happened here."

I went through it all again, arriving at the historical society, finding Grace's body, and trying to revive her. The red light on the recorder stared at me as I went through the events. I had to stop several times and wipe my eyes and blow my nose. By the time I stopped talking, my nose was reddened and my fingers were white. I tried to relax my fingers, but they kept returning to fists.

"Let's go back a bit." This from Trooper Gray. "Why were you coming to meet with Grace at the museum? It's not open yet."

I took a deep breath. "Things have disappeared from the museum. Nothing valuable, but documents and some equipment were taken between the time we closed in October and when I checked earlier this month."

Trooper Bachelor made a note on a pad of paper. Didn't the police use tablets? "That's almost eight months. You didn't notice anything missing before?"

"The museum is closed from October until June. The carriage house and the main house aren't heated, so nobody goes in there regularly."

"You don't check during the winter?" Trooper Bachelor sounded like he was scolding me for not paying attention. Or maybe that was his interviewing technique. Or maybe I was a suspect. Better stick to answering only the questions asked. After years with Todd, I knew that people got in trouble offering information.

"Not often, only about once a month. We're in the country, so I mainly check for insect and animal damage. Bats and mice come into the structures in the winter. Raccoons too, they can make a mess, tearing apart things." As if that were the most relevant part of my statement. And I'd already broken my rule not to volunteer information.

"When is the last time you were in the building? Before today?" Trooper Gray had joined the conversation again.

"A few weeks ago. I didn't notice anything missing, but the ice harvesting stuff is kept in the carriage house. We've been moving things around, making room for the Rabbit Run exhibit, so I don't know where everything is kept."

"Rabbit Run?" asked Trooper Gray.

"Yeah, it's the railroad that ran through Swift River Valley; jumped from station to station, like a rabbit. It's a new exhibit, just finished this winter." Now I sounded like a tour guide, again. But I was sticking to the questions asked. "I didn't know anything was missing until Kevin told me."

Trooper Gray made more notes. "Kevin?"

"Yeah, Kevin Angetti. He told me the equipment was missing. I went through things and found out some documents and other papers were gone too."

"When you told me things walked away, you didn't tell me about Kevin being the one to figure it out," said Gray.

"Didn't think it was important," I said.

At the same time, Bachelor asked, "Who's Kevin Angetti?"

I'd rather deal with Bachelor in this moment. "Kevin Angetti is a docent at the museum and he does some maintenance, as needed. We came out to do some spring cleaning and he noticed things missing. I'm more familiar with the documents."

"Any relation to the Angettis that own the gas station and convenience store over by the highway?" asked Gray.

"His uncle and cousins," I said. "Kevin lives with them."

Bachelor made another notation on his paper. "When did he make this discovery?"

I pulled out my phone. "We did the cleanup on April 4."

Trooper Gray leaned forward. "And what does this have to do with the meeting with Grace?"

"Grace did the premises check in March," I said. There was more to it, but I didn't want to be accusing a dead woman without evidence.

"Kevin was the last one who saw the missing items." Gray made it a statement, not a question.

"Yeah, but I'm sure he didn't have anything to do with the missing items," I said.

"How do you know that?" Gray asked. "What proof do you have that he's not involved?"

I saw black spots across my eyes. No, not now. I wanted to get through this interview without morning sickness. "Morning sickness" was a misnomer; it occurred all through the day, most often at the worst possible time. Like now.

"I need to go." I attempted to stand, but slid back into the chair.

"Just a few more questions," said Trooper Bachelor.

Gray stared at me. "Are you all right?"

The troopers looked at each other.

"I'm pregnant," I said, one more time. "And nervous." I grabbed the water bottle and took a slug. "It's okay now." I wasn't quite over it yet, but I was feeling better.

"What did Grace have to do with the missing items?" asked Gray.

"Grace is the granddaughter of Betsy Adams. In the past, Betsy and Grace accused Lillian Freeman and her family of taking things. There's bad blood between the families. But I spoke to the Adamses and to the Freemans and didn't find anything about the theft. And Lillian died last January."

"Now it's not things missing, it's a theft?" Bachelor made more notations on his pad. "Did you suspect Grace Connelly?"

"She was one of the few people with access," I said. "Can I go now?"

"Just one more thing." Trooper Gray pulled an envelope from the case on the floor.

CHAPTER THREE

"We found these under Ms. Connelly's body. They look like they belong to the historical society." She opened the envelope and placed the two clear bags on the table.

I looked at both of them. One, a letter, was already in a plastic sleeve, before it went into the evidence bag; the paper was yellow and crumbling. The other was a copy of a century-old advertisement. I recognized them.

"These are from the archives," I said. "The letter is an original, that's why it was already in a plastic sleeve. The advertisement is from flyers given out by Rufus Powers. I don't know where the original is, but this is one of many copies that were made."

I reached for the documents.

"Please don't touch them," said Bachelor. "Even if they are in evidence bags."

"You found these under Grace's body?" I asked. "They were placed there before she died?"

"You tell us," said Gray. "The photocopied document has writing on the back." She took the plastic bag and flipped it over. Someone had written, with a pencil, and it was smudged in places.

"That wasn't on any copy that I know of," I said. "It's written in pencil, but when? What does it mean? I can barely make out some of the writing. It's forty-two, dash, twenty-one, dash, thirty-three. Next line is zero-seven-two, dash, eighteen, dash, zero-zero. Is it a code?"

"We don't know," said Gray. "Hoped the archivist could help us out."

She stared at me. I had no idea what the numbers met.

"There are more numbers at the bottom," I said. "They look like amounts of money, all lined up at the decimal point."

"But you've never seen the numbers before?" Gray spread them apart and pushed them closer to where I sat. "Do you suspect Ms. Connelly in the disappearance of things at the museum?"

"No." I moved my hand towards them; then remembered I wasn't supposed to touch. "The letter looks like an original. We have an almost complete set of correspondence between Rachel Bauman and her friend, Louisa Ames. They talk extensively about life in the valley as the dam was being built. They aren't worth a great deal of money, but they are irreplaceable."

"Were some of these letters missing?" Trooper Gray scooped them up and put them back into the envelope. "Were these the letters you wanted to talk to Grace about?"

"No." I pulled the chair toward the table. "The missing documents are mostly business records, requests for logging, clearing of land, and ice harvesting. They all have something to do with businesses run by Grace's family."

"Why are these letters with Grace?" asked Gray. "Was she working on them?"

"Not that I know of." Though there was a lot I didn't know about Grace. "Louisa and Rachel talked about their boyfriends, town politics, and, in this letter, the burning of the Enfield church."

"The burning of the church?" This from Bachelor.

"Yes, arson was suspected. Just days before the church was due to be demolished, it was destroyed by fire. The society has several pictures, taken at the time of the damage. Some other buildings burned just before they were supposed to be torn down, but the Enfield church is the most famous." Here I was doing my tour guide thing again. But it was familiar, and I was hoping it would keep me from thinking about Grace, lying dead in the next building. Damn, now I couldn't get that picture out of my mind. "These documents make me believe that Grace's death had something to do with her grandmother and her quest for justice."

Gray tapped the documents, though she'd just told me not to touch them. "Do you have any idea why they would be under Grace's body?"

"No." I found myself playing with my hair. A sure sign I was nervous. "But Grace was Rachel Bauman's great-grand-niece."

Gray leaned forward. "How did that work?"

"Grace's grandmother, Betsy Adams, is Rachel Bauman's sister. That's why Grace's death must be connected to the documents. Grace was certain that her family businesses had been taken from them by nefarious means. She was always trying to prove that the family had been taken advantage of."

"The same Betsy Adams that is feuding with Lillian Freeman?" Trooper Gray was asking the questions, but Bachelor was still taking notes.

"Yes. But I'm sure it's a coincidence." There were less than a thousand people in New Salem. It was unlikely.

"We'll look into that," said Gray. "Did you suspect Ms. Connelly in the disappearance of things at the museum?"

The abrupt change of topic stopped me for a moment. "No." I didn't sound convincing, even to myself. "But Grace was one of a handful of people that had keys and access in the winter. I wanted to talk to her about what she saw and what she knew."

"Who else did you suspect?" asked Bachelor.

"I didn't suspect anyone," I said. "But the only people with keys were Grace; Irene, the administrative assistant; Kevin Angetti, the maintenance person; and me."

"Kevin Angetti again," said Bachelor.

"Looks like we need to talk to him," said Gray. "We'll need contact information on all of them."

"They're not suspects," I said. "Nothing in the museum is worth a great deal, except to the people directly concerned. Taking these letters, that's personal. It had to be someone who knew Grace."

"All death is personal," Bachelor said. "Now tell us about Kevin Angetti."

"What about Kevin?" I asked.

"You said he discovered the missing items," said Gray. "Could he have taken them?"

"For what reason?" I asked. "Kevin likes old things, and history, but he has no direct connection to Grace or her family. He's a part-time docent and maintenance person, as needed."

"Maybe he didn't know the value of the items he took," said Gray. "This is a museum; maybe he thought they were valuable."

I had to get them off the topic of Kevin. He was just a kid, trying to be helpful, and they were accusing him of stealing. "Kevin's been at the museum for years," I said. "If he is a thief, and I don't believe that, why did he take so long to remove what he wanted?"

Gray and Bachelor looked at each other.

"We're exploring all the possibilities," said Gray.

"In my opinion, you should spend more time on the historical connections." I stared at Gray, willing her to believe me. "The fact that you found these documents under Grace must mean something." I felt like I was repeating myself, but the troopers didn't seem to get the connections between Grace's death and her family history.

"Yeah, well, you're an archivist," said Bachelor.

"And you're investigators," I shot back a little too quickly. It didn't matter though, because they didn't care about my opinion.

"Please get us the information on people who had access and who argued with Grace," said Gray. "The sooner the better."

"Can I go now?" I was exhausted.

"I guess that's it." Bachelor picked up his pad and the envelope and put them into the file case. "We know where you are if we have more questions."

We got to the top of the stairs before we were stopped by another trooper.

Miss Rachel Alice Bauman
43 Turnpike Road
Enfield, Massachusetts

August 3, 1936
Dear Louisa:

The Enfield church burned down last night. We are just down the road and I woke up when the Dana fire truck went by. It has got an engine and makes more noise than the horse-drawn fire truck of Enfield. I got dressed and went outside. It seems the entire town was there, as it was a warm night. Someone managed to get the communion table out of the church and it was sitting in the road when I arrived.

Sitting on the table, big as day, was Molly Evers, the woman who runs the boarding house in town. She was swinging her legs and talking to the young men who stay with her. My mother says she's not a nice woman and she has been to the Orange courthouse, accused of serving more than food to the men staying there. She was released, and the charges dismissed, just last month. And now she's sitting on the communion table. You could see her legs and her black stockings.

We have been having meetings about the church for over a year. The Metropolitan District Commission, the people in charge of taking down houses and building dams for the new reservoir, say that everything will be underwater in a few years. The Board of Trustees had a meeting about moving the church to another location, but they could not agree on which town it should be relocated to and still allow its members to attend. Then the Board talked to other area churches, to give them items such as the communion set and the bells. Many items have been removed and, Papa said, the Trustees seemed to have accepted that the church will be destroyed.

Someone burned it before the Trustees could act. Papa says that many people in town were angry enough to do the deed, but the local constabulary doesn't have any definite idea who did it. Many men are walking around town today, with notebooks and pencils, interviewing everyone who lives here. Nothing remains but the communion table and a few other things that people got out of the church.

Albert and I had talked about being married in that church. Now, don't go spreading rumors, he hasn't proposed or given me a ring. We just talk about getting married sometime, as we have known each other since we were children. He has got a good job now, running a crew that is cutting down trees around Mount Zion. Governor Curley (Papa says he's a Democrat) put lots of Irish to work doing forestry in the Swift River Valley. I guess they do not have trees in Ireland, because most of the men don't know what they are doing. Albert and some other local people head the crews and teach the Irish how to cut down a tree without killing or maiming themselves or others. Albert has some problems, as he is younger than most of the crew leaders, but at least he knows which end of the axe cuts and how to swing it.

But now we can't get married in Enfield. The Prescott church is being moved, but Dana still has a Congregational Church. Of course, St. Anne's is there too, but that's where all the Irish Papists go. I've never set foot in that church and have no desire to do so. We may have to leave the valley to get married.

I guess we are all going to have to leave the valley soon.

With greatest affection,
Rachel

NOTICE

Greenwich Village, Mass, August 1925

The subscriber would respectfully inform all who are engaged in the manufacturing of Carriages, that he still continues to manufacture

SPOKES

Of all sizes, and will supply all orders remarkably cheap for cash. Anyone who may be in want of the above article, if they will inform him by mail or otherwise, can be supplied at their shops, or have them left at the most convenient place nearby, but he would prefer to have customers call at his shop and select for themselves. Said shop is about 2 ½ miles north of Greenwich Village.

ARTICLES TAKEN IN EXCHANGE FOR SPOKES

All kinds of grain, Neat stock, Sheep, Wool, Leather, and some Harnesses, and in some cases a part or all in store pay. Also occasionally a nice Horse or Carriage, but for the first quality of timber, cash will be expected generally. Just give us a call, and you shall be supplied so cheap that you will find it to your profit to call again. Small orders from a distance cannot always be answered.

Most respectfully yours,
Rufus Powers

CHAPTER FOUR

The troopers whispered at the top of the stairs. The newcomer, the trooper I didn't know, had my lanyard and was gesturing outside. He showed something—another document I think—to Bachelor, who added it to his file box.

Fatigue caught up with me. I struggled to stand up straight and I thought I heard the troopers talking about peanut butter. And where the hell was Todd? He should've gotten out of work and heard my message over an hour ago. It only took half that time to get from the house of correction to New Salem. We'd done some quarrelling lately, mostly about my pregnancy, but he'd stand by me if I needed help. And he was the chief of police.

I was exhausted and disgusted and trying not to freak out about finding Grace's dead body. I took a series of deep breaths and concentrated on what I needed to do next. I started toward the door of the church.

"Miss Wetherby, please wait a moment." This from the trooper I didn't know, though he'd taken the time to figure out who I was.

"I want to go home." I was doing the whining thing again, but now I didn't care.

"Emma, please come to the barn with us." Now Trooper Gray and I were on a first-name basis.

"I'm sorry, what is your first name?" I looked at Trooper Gray. "Now that we're being informal."

To my surprise, she answered the question. "It's Loretta. I know that you're tired and may be overwhelmed, but we need your help again."

Archivists are helpful. If she'd threatened me, or bullied me, I'd fight back. But I'd been through volumes of paper and knew where things were. "What do you want me to do?"

"I'm Trooper Wilson," said the newcomer. "You can call me Carl. And I want you to check out something in the barn."

All of us left the church and walked past the carriage house to the barn. The carriage house was still open and I could see the 1929 Dana fire truck; no troopers appeared to be in the building.

"Great Model A firetruck," said Carl. "Does it run?"

"Yes," I said. "We take it out for special events, such as Old Home Days. It's temperamental, but it runs."

"I'd love to work in a place like this." Carl was chatty, though he probably had no idea what it took to keep a rural museum running. "Are you hiring?" he asked.

"No," I said. "Not unless you have fundraising experience. It's just me and a part-time administrator. We pay the docents a forty-five-dollar stipend for a three-hour shift. No money to kill for."

That last statement was uncalled for, but I wanted to go home.

"That's too bad," said Carl. "How long has this place been here?"

"The historical society was formed in 1938 to preserve the records of Dana, Enfield, and Greenwich, the towns that were flooded by the Quabbin. The artifacts were originally kept at the New Salem Library. The museum later acquired the Whitaker-Clary House and moved here." This was a speech I'd given hundreds of times. So had Grace. I pushed her from my mind. "The town of Prescott originally had its own historical society in the church that was moved from Prescott to Orange. In 1984, that historical society combined with Swift River and the church was moved to this location."

"And the barn and the carriage house?" Carl seemed genuinely interested.

"The barn came with the house. The carriage shed was built in the 1990s to fit in with the style of the museum."

"What's in the barn now?" This from Trooper Gray. We were standing in front of the door by this time.

"Not much," I said. "There's some stuff stored in there. The floor is rotted in places and it's not safe to walk on."

"Well, somebody's been in here." Trooper Wilson opened the door. I peered into the darkness and could make out a lantern, a sleeping bag, and a jar of peanut butter on the floor.

"Those things don't belong." I stepped toward the barn. "It looks like somebody is living here."

Trooper Gray stood in front of me. "Please stay out of the building."

I backed up.

"Emma, what's going on?" said a familiar voice. "I came as soon as I got your message."

Everyone turned to face Todd, who had arrived at last. He had changed out of his uniform, but he still stood like a cop, shoulders back, and he flashed his badge. "Todd Mitchell, chief of police, New Salem. I got a 911 call about a homicide. And Emma left me a message."

Trooper Gray moved from the barn to stand in front of Todd. "I'm Trooper Gray. I'm in charge of this scene. We were about to notify you."

Trooper Gray was good at the "I'm in charge" stance. Even I knew that the state police conducted all homicide investigations, outside of the major cities. New Salem had two part-time officers, and no detectives. But Todd wasn't backing down.

"I should have been notified right away," Todd said. "I know the people involved."

Everyone stayed in place for several moments.

I went to Todd and took his arm. "I'm so glad you're here. I was worried when I couldn't reach you."

"I turned off my phone at work," said Todd, as he took the opportunity to step away. "I just turned it back on and came directly here."

"Sir, do you know this woman?" asked Trooper Bachelder.

I found a tissue, wiped my eyes, and blew my nose. "He's the father of my child," I said.

CHAPTER FIVE

Everyone stared at me for a moment.

"Chief Mitchell is your husband?" Trooper Gray emphasized the last word.

"He is the father of my child," I said. "We're talking about getting married." As I was talking to a state trooper, I thought it was important to be precise.

"What's going on here?" Todd asked.

Trooper Bachelor took out his notebook. "There's a body in the house. Your..." He waved his hand in the air. "Your partner found it earlier today."

"Emma, are you alright? What happened?"

"I was supposed to meet Grace this afternoon. I got here and found her on the floor." I felt myself tearing up again. I swallowed, wiped my eyes again, and continued. "I tried CPR, I tried to revive her, but she was already dead."

Todd looked at Gray. "You're in charge?"

"I am. We've cleared the scene, only us and authorized personnel on the premises. You may have a conflict here, chief. We'll have to deal with that."

I knew enough about police procedure to know there was no "may have" about the conflict. I lived with Todd, I found Grace's body, and he was not going to be allowed to run the investigation. Whether he got to participate at all was up to the state police.

"What about somebody living in the barn?" Trooper Gray asked.

Everyone turned their attention to the open door, with the sleeping bag and the jar of peanut butter on the floor. Trooper Gray took a few steps into the barn and looked around.

"Nobody here now," she said. "But we'll take everything here as evidence, as soon as the crime scene techs get here." She turned to face Todd and me. "And I need to ask Emma about another document." She reached into the file box again and came up with another plastic sleeve. "We found this in the barn."

I recognized it also. "How are all these historic documents leaving the archives room and I don't know anything about it? Some of these things are one of a kind and they end up in the barn and under Grace." I couldn't catch my breath. My mouth and nose were full of mucus and I tried to force air into my lungs. The black dots were back and I felt dizzy. "And Grace is dead." I started crying again.

Todd put his arm around me and took me to the nearest place to sit, the back steps of the Whitaker-Clary House. I sat and tried to collect myself. He gave me some tissues and I wiped my eyes and blew my nose. Rocked back and forth on the steps until the baby and I were comfortable.

"You recognize this document." Trooper Gray didn't even phrase it as a question.

"Let her have a minute," said Todd.

I was so lucky to have him. He cared about me and the baby, even if he sometimes had trouble showing it. And I was tired of being the strong one and was more than ready for him to take over. I took several calming breaths and savored the feel of oxygen spreading through my body.

I heard another vehicle and looked up to see a long, black car enter the driveway. On its side it proclaimed "Commonwealth of Massachusetts, Office of the Medical Examiner."

"Let's get out of here." I stood up.

"Just a minute." Trooper Gray held the document in the evidence sleeve out to me. "Please identify this."

I turned the sleeve over, but I knew what it was and where it came from. "It's another letter."

"We know that." Trooper Gray let her exasperation show. "Is it part of your collection?"

"Yes, it's another letter from Rachel Bauman to a friend. There are several of them in the collection. By the wear and the fact that it's in a Mylar wrapping, I'd say it's one of ours. Where did you find it?"

"In the barn." Trooper Wilson returned the document to the file box. "You said it's yours. Are there other letters that are not at the museum?"

"Will I get these things back? They're important to the collection."

"Of course," said Trooper Gray. "Do you have any idea how it got in the barn?"

"I don't have any idea why any of this is happening." And I didn't like the feeling of being out of control. I needed to know more about Grace and her family. But not tonight. Tonight, I just wanted to sleep. "Can we go now?"

"First, you need to answer my question." Trooper Gray put her feet apart and rested her hands on her belt. "Are there other letters that are not in the museum? Where are they?"

"Betsy Adams has some of the letters. They were written by her sister, Rachel, and some are still at the house," I said.

"The house that she shared with Grace Connelly?" Trooper Gray leaned toward me. "Are you sure it's not one of hers?"

"Yes, I'm sure. I'm the archivist; I know what's in our collection and what's not." Trooper Gray had me doubting my own knowledge, but I didn't want her to know that.

"We have an appointment," said Todd. "We need to leave. You can ask more questions later."

Todd led me to the parking lot.

Miss Rachel Alice Bauman
43 Turnpike Road
Enfield, Massachusetts

March 30, 1936
Dear Louisa:

 I sat in the balcony at the Enfield town meeting, with the other ladies, while the Selectmen and town officials went on about eminent domain and takings for fair value. Much of it was boring, but Papa said I had to attend, as he was the town treasurer and it wouldn't be proper if I failed to appear. They talked about Governor Curley at the town meeting for over an hour. Most of the men of the town are Republicans, who believe that the town should look out for its own, without outside interference. Governor Curley sides with the Irish, who think that the government should take care of them. In Boston, he spent money on beaches and playgrounds. Several years ago, his own party refused him a place in the Massachusetts delegation to nominate Franklin Roosevelt (another Democrat). He can't even get along with his own party, and now he's trying to take our valley.
 When my father gave his treasurer's report, I had some sympathy with the position of the Democrats. Papa went through the amounts given to each of the town employees over the last year, including $14 for the person ringing the church bells and $72 for the schoolmaster. Then he came to the allowances for widows. Most families got $10 to $20 a year for taking a woman into their home. They allotted $7 to bury the widow Loretta Pike. I hope I never have to live off what the town gives to me.

The Swift River Box Factory has closed its doors; it is unclear when and whether it will ever reopen. Mama, Betsy, Alma, and I made money during the winter months weaving the fronds of palm into hats. Mr. Gowey brought us the fronds and took away the finished hats, and the factory paid us for each completed one. Of course, we didn't add hatbands or feathers; that was done somewhere else.

The appearance of Mr. Gowey was the highlight of a dreary winter week. He arrived with his two draft horses, one gray and one white, plodding along and dragging the sleigh behind him. The sleigh was piled high with palm fronds, many of them flopping in the back. By the time he got to our house, the front seat was covered with finished hats. It is hard to believe that enough people need hats each year that we kept producing them and they kept getting sold. They're good hats too, closely woven, so they don't wear out. If the hats weren't woven closely enough, Mr. Gowey won't take them and we didn't get paid. I had a few left behind in the beginning, but I got better at it. I learned that I couldn't wait until the night before he came and try to make up for my slothfulness during the week. I needed to weave every night in front of the fire. The palm cuts into my hands, so weaving every night was painful. I kept a jug of lanolin water, left over from washing the sheep's wool, by my side. It softened my hands and seemed to make the palm fronds bend more easily.

Last winter was the last of the hat weaving and, this coming winter, there will be a significant loss of income. Now we must rely on the farm and my papa cutting ice in the winter. He's talking of having Betsy, Alma, and I help in the ice cutting, as he has no sons. I did it once, and the wind whipped across the pond, freezing my fingers and my legs.

The saw is clumsy and hard to handle, and I can't lift the blocks of ice from the pond. It is nice in the summer, when the ice in the icebox allows us to have cold milk on a hot day.

I hope this letter finds you well and happy. Please write back and tell me about your family and their new life in Pelham.

With endless affection,
Rachel

CHAPTER SIX

We were both silent until we got to the car. Todd kept his arm around me, though I assured him that my dizziness had passed. He got into the driver's seat and started the ignition.

"Thank you for getting me out of there." I fastened my seatbelt. "I can't wait to get home, take a hot bath, and go to bed."

"We're having dinner tonight with Brian and Dierdre." He put the car in drive and we started off down the road. "What are we going to feed them? Or do you want to go out?"

"Oh, shit. I'd forgotten about them. Can we postpone it?"

Todd turned to stare at me. It was a rural road; we were the only people on it, but still. "Keep your eyes on the road."

"They said they wanted to talk to us about something important," Todd said.

He was right; those were almost their exact words. I didn't want to do this, but they were Todd's kids. Well, Dierdre was his daughter and Brian was his stepson, the child of his former wife, Carol. Todd had enough issues with starting another family when his first two children were adults without my cancelling this dinner that had taken weeks to set up. I'd planned to get home early and do a pork roast, one of Brian's favorite dishes. It was still in the freezer. Why did I have to be in charge of everything?

"I don't feel like getting dressed up and going out." My first line of defense was always addressing only the question Todd asked. "Let's stop at the general store and see what they have. It's not pizza night, is it?"

"Pizza night is Friday. Not today."

Todd's first line of defense was stating the obvious.

"And don't tell them about the pregnancy," Todd added.

We'd been through this discussion before. I had a medical appointment the next day; it would be the first time he came with me. He insisted we not tell his children until afterward. I knew I was pregnant and saw no point in pretending I wasn't.

Todd reached across the console to take my hand. "I know you've had a rough day. And I know I'm sometimes difficult to live with. But thanks for doing this."

"They're going to know before long. My clothes are getting tight."

"I just want the time to be right. They have something important to tell us, let's just concentrate on that tonight." Todd pulled into the parking lot of the New Salem Country Store.

That might be the best plan. Other than family gatherings and holidays, this was the first time I remembered them asking for a family meeting to discuss something. We went into the store, where the smell of corn chowder permeated the room. We bought a gallon (it was good left over), some bread, and salad fixings. Todd checked out the bakery and got a chocolate cake for dessert; it was a favorite of his and Brian's.

"I need to tell them about what happened at the historical society. About Grace."

"Why?" asked Todd. "Can't we just have a pleasant evening?"

"Todd, I found a dead body today. The first dead body I've ever seen, other than on satin during calling hours. And I'm pregnant and keeping it a secret. Brian is a little dense, like you, but Dierdre will wonder why I'm an emotional mess. They need an explanation."

"Does it make you feel better to call me dense?"

"Yes, it does." I smiled, the first time in hours. "And thank you for not making me elaborate on the dead body." I blinked away the tears. Not here and now.

Still no offer to postpone because of my feelings. That was the dense part.

We got home about a half hour before the children were expected. They weren't children, but I called them that because Todd did. My own personal statement, as I was only nine years older than Brian. Barney, the wonder dog, greeted us at the door. I gave him fresh water and fed him supper. He went to flop in the corner. Todd said he would take care of the food while I went to lie down for a few minutes and got myself together. Before I left, I reminded Todd that Barney would need to be put in the shed; he had a dog bed there for when Dierdre came to visit. She was allergic to dogs and Barney shed lots of hair.

The slamming of the door and footsteps let me know that our visitors had arrived. I put on some mascara and lip gloss and checked myself in the mirror. Some tiny brown dots trailed across the leg of my pants. Probably blood. That didn't upset me as much as I thought it would, but I changed my clothes anyway. Left the shirt and pants soaking in cold water in the bathroom sink. I'd deal with the stains later.

As I came down the stairs, I heard Todd telling Brian and Dierdre that I wasn't feeling well. He said I'd found a body that afternoon at the society and it had taken a lot out of me. No mention of my pregnancy. I saw no reason to keep it a secret, but Todd wanted to wait to tell his children. Though after today, it would probably be the talk of the town. I hope he didn't wait too long.

I entered the kitchen, where the three of them had gathered. "I'm feeling much better now. Do you need help with the meal?"

All three turned to look at me. Todd had a wine bottle in his hand and three glasses on the counter.

"Dad was just pouring wine," said Brian. "Do you want some?" He got up and took another glass out of the cupboard.

"None for me," I said.

"Me neither," said Dierdre. She turned to me. "Are you sure? It will calm your nerves."

But it probably wouldn't do much for the baby. The baby we weren't talking about. "I'll just have seltzer water. It'll settle my stomach."

"Dad was telling us what happened to you," said Dierdre. "Was it awful?" She shook her head and waved her hand. "That's not what I meant. I'm sure it was awful. Are you sure you're up to having us here?"

This was my chance to cut the evening short, to go back upstairs and just lie on the bed and stare at the ceiling. "No, it's fine. I have to eat anyway, and I want to hear your big news."

Todd filled two glasses and we took them into the living room. Brian and Dierdre sat on the love seat together and Todd and I took the armchairs. Nobody seemed to want to start the conversation.

"Are you going to be investigating the murder at the museum?" Dierdre asked.

"Not likely," said Todd. "Emma found the body and that means I have a conflict."

"Something finally happens in New Salem and you don't get to be a part of it?" Brian stopped talking and looked at the floor. "That sounds horrible, I know. Do you know the woman who died?"

"She's a docent at the museum. Emma knows her," Todd said. "I went to school with her, but haven't seen her for years."

"Can we talk about something else?" I asked.

Todd took it upon himself to change the topic. "Tell us how you've been doing now that both of you are living in Boston. Do you see each other regularly?"

"That's what we came out to talk to you about," said Brian. "Our plans."

"You're making plans together?" Todd took a sip of wine. "I thought you were taking water samples and Dierdre was selling pastries."

The two of them looked at each other, then down at the floor. Brian was an environmental engineer; he did significantly more than take water samples. Dierdre sold software and social media services to restaurants, bars, and bakeries. Todd often downplayed their jobs and education, but neither of them had ever looked uncomfortable with his teasing before.

"Dad, you know we both have good jobs." Brian reached out and took Dierdre's hand. "We both make more than you do."

Now it was Todd's turn to look at the floor. Not that Brian's statement wasn't true.

"I have an important job," said Todd, "even if I don't get a chance to investigate Grace's death."

"We know," said Brian, "but what we do is important too. And we're making plans for the future."

"What plans?" asked Todd. "Either of you in a relationship? Going to make me a grandfather?" Todd sipped the wine. "Of course, I'm way too young to be a grandpa."

I looked at Todd, hoping for him to announce my pregnancy. My mouth opened, then closed. These were his kids; he needed to do it on his time. Todd remained silent.

"That's what we want to talk to you about," said Dierdre.

"You're getting married." Todd leaned forward into his seat. "You've met the love of your life."

"Not like you think," said Dierdre.

"Nothing's going like I think," said Todd. "Just today, I've been at the scene of a murder and found Emma right in the middle of it. I'd looked forward to a dinner with you two. What's going on?"

"We didn't come here for the food," said Brian. "We came to see you."

"I know that." Todd put his wine glass on the side table. "But it's been a day of surprises. Tell me yours."

Brian moved closer to Dierdre, though they were both jammed on the love seat. "Dierdre and I are getting married."

The silence piled up in the corners. Todd leaned back in his chair, staring at his daughter and his stepson.

Brian took Dierdre's hand, already in his, and pulled it onto his lap. "We've been attracted to each other since high school," he said. "But this last year, we realized we wanted to stay together forever."

"But you're brother and sister. Siblings don't get married," Todd said.

I wasn't sure this was the right thing to say, but I kind of agreed with Todd. Brian and Dierdre had been twelve years old when Todd married Brian's mother, so they had grown up together. I thought about my feelings for my brother; romance was never a part of our relationship. He was my biological brother, but still, this bothered me.

"We're not siblings," said Brian. "And we are going to get married."

"When is the wedding?" I asked. They struck me as the type of couple that would want a huge blowout wedding, one that would take a year or more to plan. Lots could happen in a year.

Todd got up, went into the kitchen, and came back with the rest of the bottle of wine.

I saw black dots before my eyes. My pregnant body was betraying me again.

"Let's talk about this," I said. "What plans have you made?"

"Emma, are you alright?" Dierdre got up and came over to stand by me. "You're awfully pale and you slurred your words."

"It must be a delayed reaction to the murder," I said. "It's thrown me off my game." I glared at Todd, willing him to say something. He ignored me. "Tell me about your plans."

"We've put a deposit down on a house," said Dierdre. "We're supposed to close at the end of May."

Whoa. That sounded permanent and committed. Todd still hadn't said anything and was staring at the wine in his glass. Like he was trying to decide whether to drink it or to strangle Brian.

"Buying a house," said Todd. "That sounds serious."

"We are serious," said Dierdre. "And we're planning to get married in July."

"July of this year?" Todd started pacing back and forth across the living room. Eight steps and turn. Eight steps and turn. Our living room wasn't that large. "Why the rush?"

Dierdre took a deep breath and let it out with an audible sigh. In an ominous moment, I knew what was coming next.

"Dad," said Dierdre. "I'm pregnant."

Todd stopped pacing. "And it's Brian's kid?" He had on his "cop face," the one that shut out the world. Never play poker with him.

"Of course it's mine," said Brian. "We're going to be parents in November. How could you even ask that, after what we've told you?"

One month after I was due, Todd would have a grandchild just one month younger than his child. He'd be a pop-grandpop. I muffled a giggle that escaped before I could stop it.

Todd turned to me. "You think this is funny?"

I didn't say anything. I wanted to get up and move around but was afraid my legs wouldn't support me.

"I wanted you to know first, before we told anyone else," said Dierdre. "There's a whole part of our life that we haven't let you see, and I wanted it to stop. Don't you think we should share the big events in our life?"

"You told me first? You haven't told your mother?" Todd stopped pacing and confronted Brian.

Brian stood up. "Of course we told her. She was the first, but you are a close second. I hope you are happy for us."

"I need to talk to Carol." Todd put down his glass and looked around, as if he were going to call Carol, Brian's mother, immediately. "What did she say about your plans?"

"She's happy for us," said Dierdre. "It's difficult to find someone special and, with Brian, we've already worked out the living together part."

"As brother and sister," said Todd. "Not as a married couple. And not as parents."

"Mom is happy for us. Why can't you be too?" This from Dierdre, who looked anxiously from Todd to Brian.

"It's a lot to take in," said Todd. "I've always thought of you as my children, but now it's a whole other experience. I thought families shared things."

That was the surprising subtext of this conversation. We knew about the events in their lives, but Todd still didn't share the news of my pregnancy. He made fists of both hands and held them at his side. He was trying hard not to say what he was thinking. He resumed pacing.

"I've barely gotten used to the idea that you are both adults, now I'm going to be a grandfather," said Todd. "Double."

"Excuse me." I hurried out of the room and barely made it to the toilet before getting sick. Good thing I'd only had seltzer water. I sat on the toilet seat and waited for the dizziness to pass.

When I returned to the living room, Dierdre and Brian had their coats on. "Aren't you staying for dinner?" I pointed to the food, set out on the table.

"No," said Brian. "I think we should leave. Give you a chance to think about what was obviously a shock to you."

Dierdre went over to Todd and put her hand on his arm. "Once, you said that you would love me no matter what I did. I hope that's still true."

Todd threw back his shoulders and stared past Dierdre's head. He didn't say anything.

I walked to the door with them. "I'll call you," I said. "We can work this out. I'm sure your father will come around."

Todd continued to stand and stare as they left the house.

The car started and drove away.

"You should've told them you loved them," I said.

"They were raised together. They're brother and sister." Todd went over, picked up the empty wine bottle, and put it in the recycle bin. He took another bottle off the shelf.

I wasn't sure alcohol was the solution to this problem, but I didn't have a better idea.

"Would you want to marry your brother?" Todd asked.

I thought of my brother, with his stints in rehab and his criminal record. Though I loved him, I made it a point not to get tangled in his life. "No." I didn't want to get involved with my sister, either, but that was a different story.

"And what were you doing, laughing?" Todd continued.

It took me a second to remember. "I was imagining your child and grandchild being the same age. Growing up together."

"Maybe they'll get married too." Now Todd was just being difficult. "But thanks for not mentioning your pregnancy. It was a good idea not to discuss it."

I didn't agree with him, but I didn't have anything else to say. I got Barney out of the shed and brought him upstairs, leaving Todd to put away the food from our uneaten meal.

CHAPTER SEVEN

I lay in bed and listened to Todd rattle around in the kitchen. The gruesome sight of Grace, lying on the floor with her head bashed in, would not go away. I didn't want to be alone, but I didn't want to talk to Todd when he was upset. The troopers had asked some questions about Kevin, but I couldn't believe that the quiet docent had hit anyone, especially Grace, who had taken extra time to talk to him about rural life eighty years ago. Not that Grace had first-hand knowledge, but her grandmother was the go-to person for local lore.

I must have made some noise, for Barney left his dog bed in our room and came over to stand next to the bed. I ran my fingers through his long hair. "Was somebody living in the barn, maybe for weeks or for months? They could have been watching me when I arrived at the society and wondered what I was doing when I lost my shoe. Maybe the killer was watching Grace before today." Barney didn't have an opinion he expressed, but he did put his head under my arm when I stopped patting him.

I called Irene, the administrative assistant. She agreed to make arrangements for a secure lock on the barn and to have the alarm company come out and recheck the system. That done, I felt better about returning to the historical society.

The troopers didn't seem much interested in Grace's past. They asked about the documents, of course, but I had the impression that they were checking off items. They didn't seem to realize the importance of the letter found under her body, or the fact that she was related to the person who wrote it. The troopers targeted Kevin and his family of misfits and barely paid attention to the history. I'd call them in the morning and try to impress on them the importance of history in the thefts and the murder at the historical society.

Though I'd been exhausted just a few hours ago, the thoughts crowding my mind wouldn't let me sleep. I turned over on my side. Barney walked to the other side of the bed, still looking at me. When I moved, I felt my passenger shift. "Did you feel that, Barney? Would you like a baby to play with?"

Was he or she moving in sympathy with me? What would it be like to have a child only a few weeks older than Todd's grandchild? Todd was still reluctant to talk about marriage, even though I thought it was important for parents to commit to each other. But lots of women had children before marriage and it seemed to work out. This baby grew and changed almost daily. Could I be a single mother, if that was the path my life took? What was I thinking? Todd said he would help me raise the child and he was a man of his word. But we had different ideas about what that life should be.

I heard him come up the stairs and enter the room. I turned to face him. Barney went to his corner and lay on the dog bed. He knew who'd put him into the shed earlier that night.

"Not even the dog wants to be with me." Todd took off his shirt. "You wait up for me?"

"No," I said. "The baby is restless. Do you want to feel him or her?"

Todd sat on the bed and pulled off his shoes. "I think I've heard enough about babies this evening. I just want to sleep."

I reached out to him. "You should've told Dierdre you loved her, no matter what."

"I know." He got up and placed his shoes in the closet and hung up his shirt. No clothes on the chairs and shoes kicked in the corner for him. "But what am I supposed to do? Walk her down the aisle and give her to the man I regard as my son?"

"Yes." But this time I couldn't simply answer only the question he asked. "They're not biologically related. The baby will be fine."

"I know that." Todd pulled down his pants, removed the belt, rolled it up, and placed it in the drawer. "But I thought I'd no longer have to deal with Carol, my ex, but now she'll be Dierdre's mother-in-law *and* Brian's mother. Old resentments will be dug up. And then there's you and the new baby."

I sat up in bed. "Everyone will know about my baby soon. We'll have to tell them."

"Yeah, but tonight wasn't the right time." Todd hung his pants on a hanger. "I don't know whether there will be a right time. Let's wait until the results of the testing tomorrow."

"The doctor said that testing was just routine. We're both healthy and have no family histories that were concerning."

"But you're still worried," said Todd. "You worry about everything. I bet you've made a list of questions and concerns."

"Made it yesterday," I said. "So, is the solution not to tell them and just wait until they notice?"

My voice must have sounded strained, for Barney raised his head and looked around. Seeing nothing unusual, he lowered his head to his paws.

"I don't have any answers." Todd pulled back the covers and climbed into bed. "Let's just go to sleep." He lay down and turned away from me.

I stared at the ceiling for what seemed like hours.

CHAPTER EIGHT

I woke to darkness, with the sound of Todd pulling on his pants. I heard the sound of a zipper and the sliding of the belt. No, not total darkness, the sun was trying to break through the window.

"What time is it?" Looking over at the clock on the nightstand didn't tell me anything; it was too dark to see its face.

"About seven." Todd turned on the light. "I was trying not to wake you, but it looks like that didn't work. I put Barney out in the yard."

"I don't know what woke me." I watched Todd pull on his shirt. He was still in shape, worked out every day, and it showed. He was tall, just over six feet, with broad shoulders.

"I'll let Barney in before we go and give him his kibble. You can stay in bed a while longer." Todd came over to the bed and kissed my forehead. "I just need to write some reports and make a few phone calls before we go to the doctor's office."

"Are we going to talk about last night?"

Todd went over to stare out the window. "Not now."

Though I'd finally fallen asleep about three in the morning, I didn't feel rested. The turmoil of the last twenty-four hours kept breaking through and images flashed in front of my eyes. Grace on the floor, troopers questioning me, Brian and Dierdre, and Todd not wanting to talk about it. I didn't have the energy for that battle right now.

"They should have the test results. The doctor can tell us whether we're having a boy or a girl," I said. "Which do you want?"

Todd continued to stare out of the window.

"I know this is a lot to take in." I sat up in bed. "Becoming parents. We'll be retiring when the baby graduates from college." I got out of bed, put on my robe, and went to the window to put my arms around Todd's waist. I needed human contact.

Todd didn't turn to me, but he put his hands over mine. "I don't care whether it's a boy or a girl, as long as it's healthy. After the appointment today, we'll call Brian and Dierdre. Tell them whether they're having a brother or a sister."

Despite what had happened, I felt a twinge of disappointment. I wanted Brian and Dierdre to be told, but I didn't like being reminded that he had done parenthood before, with a different woman.

"Maybe we can invite them to our wedding?" I hated the pleading tone in my voice.

"Let's concentrate on the baby; then we can start planning a wedding."

He needed time, time to heal. I had no choice but to assume he'd rebound this time, also. I climbed back into the bed, pulling the cotton blanket to my chin.

"I just need to know I'm not going through this alone," I said. But Todd was in the room with me and going to the doctor with me. Not like my previous, disastrous marriage. I'd gone through three rounds of infertility treatment, countless useless implants, and two miscarriages. I was in my third month after my third procedure, when Bob, my then-husband, decided he didn't want to be a father. He hit me so hard, I miscarried that baby also.

"I'm not Bob." Todd sat on the end of the bed. "I'll be here for the baby, whether we're married or not." He had an uncanny way of knowing what I was thinking. When he wasn't being dense. "Let's go talk to the doctor about this baby. After I make a few calls." He kissed me on the top of my head, got off the bed, and left the room.

The mattress felt cold, as if it missed Todd's presence as much as I did. After the miscarriages, and an ex-husband that didn't bear thinking about, I was ready for motherhood. With or without Todd, but I hoped that he would go on the journey. Dreams of being a mother started at age three, when I got my first baby doll. I would rock the baby, who I called Pansy, feed her, and tell her she could be anything she wanted to be when she grew up. My sister arrived six years later and I wanted to take care of her. When she got older, I realized I couldn't save her from her bad decisions.

I'd gotten married at twenty-one, convinced I was ready to be an adult. I was wrong. Or I picked the wrong man, one that wouldn't stand with me through fertility treatments and miscarriages. I now had a job, and a good man. The pregnancy was a surprise, but not unwanted. And I was ready for motherhood, though, at thirty-nine, I was considered a "high risk pregnancy."

I wasn't going back to sleep now, so I got up and went downstairs to the kitchen, where Todd had started the coffee pot. I poured a cup, took the pad and pencil from the shelf, and sat down at the table. Every day started with a to-do list. As today was a day off, for the doctor visit and to spend some time with Todd, the work list was shorter than usual. The historical society wasn't open today.

Barney came over and sniffed at the table. I gave him some toast Todd had left behind. The pipes vibrated through the old farmhouse when Todd turned on the upstairs faucet.

I couldn't concentrate, even when I tried to focus on the baby and the testing that took place the last time I was in the doctor's office. Routine tests, Dr. "call me Nancy" Graber said. Just a precaution because of my age. Maybe I did want to know the gender of the child. Not that it mattered, because I did believe that every child had the potential to do anything he or she wanted to do. I poured another cup of coffee and made myself some toast. Though I hated breakfast, I smeared peanut butter on the toast, for the baby.

After my shower and dressing, I found myself on my knees in the bottom of the closet, looking for a decent pair of flat shoes to wear to the doctor's office. I rummaged through a dozen pairs of heels. What made me think I needed shoes in every color of the rainbow? I found a pair of flats, in a box that said they were "granite." Good enough.

I was sitting on the bed, putting them on, when Todd came into the room. "Ready to go?"

"Just need to grab my purse," I said. The purse was tan and didn't go with my granite shoes. Oh, hell, it didn't make a difference. I put my phone and keys into the bag and followed Todd out the door.

Todd plugged his phone into the car and country music poured from the speakers. I wasn't particularly fond of that music, but it meant I didn't have to carry on a conversation, so we listened to Johnny Cash.

Todd and I approached the reception desk in the office. Sally, the receptionist with yellow corkscrew curls, was talking on the phone. She glanced up, hung up the phone, and motioned us forward.

"Emma Wetherby to see Dr. Graber." I placed my insurance card on the desk.

"Oh, yes." Sally took the card and ran it through the scanner. "I think Dr. Graber wants to talk to you, anyway." She handed the card back to me and glanced at Todd. "Are you the father of the child?"

"Yes," he said. "I'm Todd Mitchell."

"The doctor will want to talk to you too." Sally picked up the phone. "I'll let her know you are here."

We went to take a seat in the waiting room.

"What do you think that's about?" asked Todd. "Are they the marriage police?"

"I don't think that's what she wants to talk about," I said. "Probably wants to know whose insurance the baby will be on."

I crossed and uncrossed my legs, put my purse on the floor and picked it up. The many tests I'd had at my last visit worried me now that I was back in a medical office. They would determine the gender of the child, but they also tested for problems with the baby. I'd googled many of the tests, and they were for genetic or chromosomal abnormalities. We'd discussed this and, after two miscarriages, I wanted the baby and could deal with whatever happened. Probably overthinking this, as Todd often accused me of doing. Dr. Graber hadn't seemed at all worried at the last visit. I crossed and uncrossed my legs again, wondering how much longer I could do that.

Todd took my hand. "Are you uncomfortable? Do you need a bathroom?"

I shook my head. "No, I'm fine."

A short woman with dark hair with magenta spikes in it came to the door. "Emma," she said.

I got up and walked toward her. Todd followed.

"Are you the father of the child?" asked the woman with spiked hair. Her name tag said "Valerie."

"Yes, Valerie," said Todd. "Why do I keep getting that question?"

To my surprise, Valerie laughed. "Not everyone comes with the father of the child. Some have same sex partners, some come with the grandparents, so we always ask to make sure." She pointed down the hall. "Go directly into Dr. Graber's office."

At the previous visit, I got my weight checked, went into the examination room, and answered a bunch of questions. Then a physical exam. I'd never been in Dr. Graber's office before.

The office was immaculate. Dr. Graber sat behind a glass table, empty except for a pen set and a computer and monitor. No file cabinets, no diplomas. Natural light flooded in through a large window and there was a Museum of Fine Arts, Boston poster for a Monet exhibit on the opposite wall. I wondered if Dr. Graber did any actual work elsewhere.

Dr. Graber stood. "Please, sit down and make yourselves comfortable."

"Hello, Nancy," I said. "This is my partner, Todd."

Todd nodded in her general direction. "Dr. Graber."

"Please call me Nancy, as Emma does." Nancy gestured to the chairs.

Everyone sat down.

Nancy picked up the keyboard and placed it in front of her. "We need to talk."

"I thought we were here to learn the gender of the baby," said Todd.

That's right; we're here to learn about the baby. Nothing was wrong. Maybe it was twins. Or triplets. That's why the doctor was so guarded. But wouldn't that have shown up on the sonogram?

"That's one of the reasons," said Nancy. "Do you want to know?"

"Yes," I said.

Todd remained silent.

"Todd, do you want to know?" asked Nancy.

"Yes," said Todd. "But I also want to know what else you need to tell us."

Nancy tapped on her keyboard. "Your baby is a boy."

"Just one baby?" I asked.

"Yes, just one," said Nancy. "We would have, most likely, picked up on multiples on the sonogram."

I had some satisfaction in knowing I was right about that. We were going to have a little boy, who might look like Todd.

"But there is a problem," said Nancy. "Last time you were here, we did a series of tests, including a chorionic villus sampling, or CVS test."

I felt a coldness around my heart. "I know about that test," I said. "It's a test for Down syndrome." I could get through this.

"There's no easy way to say this," said Nancy. "Your child has extra 21 chromosomes, an indicator for Down syndrome."

No more cold. The burning in my chest spread to my arms and head. I leaned forward to make the sensation go away. It didn't help.

"Emma, are you going to faint?" Todd put his arms around me. "Are you all right?"

I sat up straight. "It was a bit of a shock." Damn, I felt my eyes filling with tears. No, I'd waited so long for a baby, this couldn't be happening. Flashes of Grace on the floor and the realization that she would never be a mother. I looked at Todd. He had on his "cop face" again. Not a hint of emotion.

Nancy produced a package of tissues from somewhere and handed them across the table. "Do you want a few minutes alone?"

"No," said Todd. "I want to know what this means. Will our baby be retarded?"

"Developmental delays are often a symptom of Down syndrome. As are unusual facial features." Nancy turned the computer monitor around to face us. On the monitor was a picture of a newborn with almond-shaped eyes, a round face, and a prominent jaw.

"These are the typical features of Down syndrome," said Nancy. "It may be accompanied by developmental delays, but how much of a delay can't be determined by prenatal testing." She turned the monitor to face her. "Your child has a rare form of the syndrome."

"Rare form. Does that mean he can't be helped?" Todd asked.

"No, in this case of Down syndrome, rare is actually better." Nancy pushed some papers across the desk. "There are three types of the syndrome. Trisomy 21, the most common kind, means that every cell in the person's body has three copies of chromosome 21. Another type, translocation syndrome, means that every cell has part or all of a third copy of the chromosome. Mosaic Down syndrome, the kind your child has, is the rarest."

"Mosaic syndrome?" I felt I had to say something. "It sounds pretty."

"It means that not all chromosome 21 cells will carry an extra copy," said Nancy. "Before extensive genetic testing, mosaic syndrome often went undiagnosed."

"You mean the baby will be normal?" I asked. I so hoped for normal.

"The baby will still have Down syndrome," said Nancy. "The level of disability can't be determined until after birth. Most babies have mild to moderate mental disabilities, but some have normal intelligence. Many will have the characteristic facial features, some will not."

"Can you run further tests to figure out specific issues with our baby?" asked Todd.

I was encouraged he still considered it "ours" and "a baby," though I was having problems following this conversation. Todd's voice kept fading in and out and Nancy seemed to be in full doctor mode.

"No tests are definitive," said Nancy. "I can give you written materials, and the Mayo Clinic has excellent online information about the syndrome. But the level of impairment will not be obvious or testable until after the baby is born."

I didn't feel anything, just the cold. More information would be good.

"Where can we get more information?" asked Todd, as if picking up on my thoughts.

I must have made some kind of noise, because both Nancy and Todd turned to look at me.

"Before you leave, I will give you information about the syndrome, and where to get help and support, and who to contact with questions." Nancy took a deep breath. "But there's another issue."

No, no, no. I heard the screaming in my head. I couldn't deal with any more issues. My child, my son, had Down syndrome. What now?

"Again, there's no easy way to say this," Nancy said. "Many couples choose to have the pregnancy terminated. If you want to pursue this option, it must be done soon. The CVS testing cannot be done until the tenth week, so you are already advanced in your pregnancy."

Nancy went on talking but I didn't hear her. Pregnancy terminated. They were talking about getting rid of my baby. I saw spots before my eyes.

"What do you think, Emma?" asked Todd.

I shook my head. "I'm sorry, what did you say?"

"Can I get you something?" asked Nancy. "Water or a soft drink?"

"No," I said. "Just repeat what you just said."

Nancy sighed. "We may be talking about a second trimester abortion. It's more intrusive. An outpatient procedure, but still maternal risk is higher."

"But we heard the baby's heartbeat," I said.

"Yes, the baby's heartbeat can be heard at about six weeks," said Nancy. "We had to wait before we could do the CVS testing."

"And when do we have to decide what we're going to do next?" asked Todd.

"As soon as possible." Nancy took a folder from under the keyboard. "Here is some information and phone numbers that you may need." She handed the papers to Todd. "Emma, is there anything I can do for you? You don't look well. I know this news is upsetting and not what you expected."

Trying to concentrate and absorb everything that happened, I found I couldn't focus.

"I need to think," I said. "I don't know what to do."

"I've given you a lot of information, very quickly," said Nancy. "The papers I gave Todd include support groups and therapists that specialize in these issues. You may want to contact them and talk with people who've gone through this.

"Of course, you can call me," Nancy continued. "But I may be with other patients and I do not generally return phone calls until after four. The papers I gave Todd include other people, both in this office and elsewhere, that can answer your questions when they come up."

"When can we get back to you about the next step?" asked Todd.

"I think Emma may need some time," said Nancy. "Why don't you take her home and the two of you can talk about it?"

More discussion between Todd and Nancy. I put my hand on my stomach and thought I could feel the heartbeat through my skin and clothing. I didn't even show yet, it was unlikely that I felt the heartbeat. We stood up to leave, got in the elevator, out of the building, and into the car without exchanging a word. I sat staring out the windshield, dreading the conversation to come.

"Well, what do you want to do?" asked Todd.

"I don't know." I just wanted to think about what the doctor had told me.

"The doctor said we needed to make a decision soon." Todd plugged his phone into the car, but didn't turn on the music. "I think we should talk about it."

"Me too. But not right now." I rummaged through my bag, looking for a tissue. "I need to think some more before I can talk about it."

"Okay, I'll just drive and listen to some music." Todd picked up his phone.

"Please don't. I just want some quiet time to think."

If not now, maybe I would never be a mother. But raising a child is hard, even one without a disability. I wished someone would make the decision for me.

CHAPTER NINE

I looked at Todd, clutching the steering wheel and doing his best not to look at me. Let's get home; then we could have this discussion. It wouldn't be far now, we were already on Route 202, a tree-lined county road, about a mile from home.

I didn't see the deer until it jumped, lightning fast, across the road right in front of the car. Todd punched the brakes, but the deer was swift enough to jump out of the way. A Honda came around the corner going in the opposite direction, and hit the deer head-on. I turned my head to watch the car and the deer go off the side of the road. The lane warning signal on our car started beeping as Todd pulled over.

"Did you see that?" asked Todd as he unfastened his seatbelt. "I'm going to see if I can help. You call 911." He opened the door and, in a few seconds, he was gone.

I dumped my purse out on the seat. The purple and white case bounced onto the floor. I grabbed it and dialed 911. No service. Not another car in sight. I got out of the car and walked down the highway. Traffic was nonexistent. As I walked toward the scene of the collision, the signal got only slightly stronger. But it was enough to let the dispatcher know about the accident and to tell her the number of the nearest highway marker. There was blood on the road; I hoped it belonged to the deer. It was clear where the car went off the road, as it flattened a path through the coltsfoot and the brush. An idea that I should be more frantic went through my mind, but maybe I'd used up all my panic and grief for the day.

As I knew that coltsfoot, with its distinctive leaves, often grew in marshy areas, I watched my step as I left the road. Half-walking and half-sliding, I made my way down the banking and into the brush. The car, off to the right, had hit a tree and the front end was smashed in. I walked around the marshy ground and saw that the Honda Civic was leaning into a drop-off over the brook below. The water in the brook was swollen by the spring thaw. No sign of the deer.

Todd was standing by the front window, talking to the driver, so I joined him there. An arm hung out the window. Broken glass from the windshield was scattered over the ground. A large branch from the tree had gone through the windshield but the driver, a dark-haired woman in her late twenties, was conscious and talking.

"Are you hurt?" Todd asked the woman. The airbag pressed against her face.

"What happened?" The woman turned to look at Todd. Her cheeks were covered with tiny white particles from the airbag. I recognized that face. It was my sister, Hadley.

"Where's my daughter?" Hadley asked.

I took a step closer. Not sure why my sister would be on this rural road. I must have made some noise, because she turned to look at me. "Emma? Emma, is that you?" She smiled at me.

I didn't feel like smiling. I hadn't seen my sister in years because of the brute of a man that she had married. He told me to leave the house and never return. And my sister had agreed with him.

"What are you doing here?" I asked.

Todd turned toward me. "Do you know this woman?" He looked back and forth between us. We both had heart-shaped faces and hazel eyes. My hair had an auburn tone to it, while Hadley was a true brunette.

"Emma is my sister," said Hadley. "Though we haven't seen each other for years. Not even an email." As if that were my fault. "What happened? What about my daughter?"

"You hit a deer and went off the road," I said. "Did you call your daughter?"

"I can't get out of the car," she said, pushing down the airbag. "The door won't open and I can't pull my legs out from under the dash."

Todd looked her over. "I don't see any blood," he said. "Are you having any trouble breathing?" The car was not running, so there were no warning lights or signals.

Todd turned to me. "Did you call 911?"

"On their way."

She continued pounding on the airbag. "I've got to get to my daughter. She's in the back seat."

"Daughter?" I asked. I moved to the back door and saw the car seat, with a child in it. Dressed in a one-piece outfit that my mother would have called a snowsuit, she looked very tiny. She wasn't moving, her eyes were shut, and I hoped she was sleeping. I knew Hadley had a child, but he would be school-age by now. This child was much younger. It struck me that my refusal to follow Hadley on social media meant that I didn't know anything about her life. Maybe she'd left Jim Mason.

"My name is Todd," he said. "And it's good to meet Emma's sister, though I wish the circumstances were different."

"I'm Hadley, glad to meet you." she answered. "That's my daughter, Meredith, in the back. Can you get to her?"

"She's still in her car seat." I stepped back as Todd came to peer into the back of the car.

The child woke up and started screaming. "Mama, mama!" At least she was alive and proclaiming her dissatisfaction.

"It's okay, honey. Mama's right here," said Hadley. "These nice people are trying to help us."

Meredith screeched.

"Can you bring her to me?" asked Hadley. "Let her see that I'm okay."

"I don't know. The car is on the edge of the banking, with the brook below," said Todd. "If I get in the car, the whole thing may slide into the water."

"It might slide anyway." Hadley started crying. "Please get her out. Soon."

Todd hesitated. The car didn't look stable where it had stopped. I started toward the back.

"Not you," said Todd. "I'll get the child out."

I looked at Meredith. Her face was bright red with tears and snot covered her face. "Meredith, are you all right?"

"Mama, mama."

"She can't answer that question," said Hadley. "She only says one or two words at a time."

Meredith pushed against the harness and shook the car seat. She reached out to her mother and wailed. I imagined my child sitting there, in a few years.

Todd crawled into the back seat.

"What are you doing?" asked Hadley.

"Trying to get her out." Todd's large hands fumbled with the many straps and buckles of the car seat. Meredith kept reaching for her mother, and tightening the harness, making it more difficult to unbuckle. At last, all the buckles seemed to give way at the same time, and Meredith leaped out of the baby seat and hit her head on the passenger seat in front of her. She cried even louder.

After she was freed, Meredith attempted to climb over the front seat, to her mother. When Todd tried to stop her, she started hitting him with her fists. The entire car shifted, pushing Meredith into the depression behind the passenger seat. With a creaking of metal that sounded like a sigh, the entire car slid down the banking into the stream below, taking Hadley, Meredith, and Todd with it.

I screamed. For the baby, for the father of my child, and for my feeling of helplessness. The car had stopped with the front end up on the bank but the rear seat in the stream. I slid down the banking, stopping just short of the brook and the car, with the back seat filling with dirty water. Another person wouldn't fit. I couldn't face losing Todd, and I couldn't live with myself if we lost Meredith.

Todd pulled the child from between the front and back seats. She was covered with mud and debris. Meredith tried to crawl out of the car and Todd grabbed on to her.

Todd looked behind him, at me. "I told you to stay back." He slid out of the car, grabbed the child by the collar of her snowsuit, and pulled her out of the car. Meredith saw her mother and started clawing at Todd. He pushed the child into my arms.

I put Meredith into a bear hug and brought her to the driver's side window, where she and her mother made eye contact. Meredith attempted to crawl through the broken window. Sliding down the slippery bank, I tried to keep us both dry. With some careful balancing, we could lean against the car and Meredith could see her mother.

Hadley made some soothing sounds and Meredith calmed down. She was not happy to be outside the window with me, but she stopped crying. I took tissues out of my pocket and wiped the tears off Meredith's face. Good, only a few drops of blood from the scratches.

"How old is she?" I asked.

"Just turned fifteen months," said Hadley. "Just learning to walk." She put her hands out the window and Meredith grabbed onto them.

"Is she Jim's child?" I asked. I couldn't think of another way to put the question, even if I'd wanted to.

"Yes, I'm still with Jim." Hadley answered the question I hadn't asked. "He's a good father and a good provider. You should give him another chance."

I didn't know how to answer that, so I said nothing.

Todd leaned between the front seats and ran his hand down Hadley's seat belt, to where it was attached. "I can't get the seat belt off," he said. "It may be jammed."

Both Hadley and Meredith calmed down, now that they could see each other. My back hurt again, holding the baby up to the window, but I figured Meredith needed to see her mother and I could tolerate it for a few more minutes.

"What do we do now?" I asked.

"I'm going to stay here with Hadley," said Todd. "If we stay still, I don't think the car will settle anymore."

Slick mud covered both sides and the bottom of the stream, and water now filled the back seat. I assumed Todd knew and didn't want to alarm Hadley.

"Anybody down there?" The voice boomed through the foliage.

"Yes, we need help." And I couldn't hold up Meredith much longer.

After some crashing, a police officer and Katie, the EMT from Grace's death, came down to the car.

"What's going on?" asked the police officer. "Is anybody hurt?"

"My daughter looks fine," said Hadley. "But I can't get out of the car."

The woods seemed to fill with people. Two people came down with a gurney between them. They tried to take Meredith out, but she refused to leave her mother. Todd stood beside the car and took Meredith from me. Police officers milled around for a while and then two of them left and came back with what looked like a giant crowbar. They tried to force the door and the car screamed its disapproval. More officers came to help and the door gave a final sigh and sprung open. Another EMT helped Hadley out of the car.

By this time, Meredith was screaming for her mother. Hadley reached for her daughter, though her arm hung at a strange angle. The EMT tried to evaluate both of them.

"Mother's got a broken arm, but the baby won't let go of her. From what I can tell, the baby is bruised but not seriously hurt." The EMT pulled the gurney nearer to the car. "But I'd like to get them both evaluated." He gestured to Meredith, still clinging to her mother. "Guess they'll have to share a gurney."

The EMTs gave me a blanket and I was warm for the first time in hours. Still wet clothing and wet shoes, but an improvement. I watched as the EMTs put both Hadley and Meredith on a gurney and attempted to get it through the marsh and the underbrush, back to the road. They must have had some experience in the country, because they accomplished it in a few minutes; then they loaded both in the ambulance, and left.

"Ready to go home?" Todd came over to me. "I think your sister's going to be okay. And so is her daughter."

"Don't we need to give a statement or something?"

"Prerogative of the police chief," said Todd. "I can leave someone else in charge and give a statement later. Are you doing okay?"

"I'm fine. Just want to get home. And I'm keeping the blanket." I stood up. "Did you get an address on Hadley?"

"Yeah," said Todd. "She's living out on Cooleyville Road. Been there about six months."

Hadley hadn't contacted me in the six months she'd lived only a few miles away. I didn't know whether to be relieved or angry. Family was difficult. Todd put his hand around my waist and helped me through the mud and underbrush to the car. I picked up my purse, still on the floor where I'd left it.

Todd got into the driver's seat. "I don't know about you," he said, "but I could use a drink."

"I can't drink," I said. "I'm pregnant.

I realized I had made my decision.

CHAPTER TEN

The next morning, I woke to a quiet house. Todd was gone, but he left me a message that he'd let Barney out for a walk. He hadn't made coffee, so that was my first task of the day. I sat at the table and made my daily to-do list. I wanted to speak with the troopers again, but before I could take any action on that, I got a phone call from Trooper Gray, asking if she could come by today. I made an appointment for one o'clock at the historical society; I could get in some research before she appeared.

Anything to avoid dwelling on the news about the baby. I longed to call someone to talk. Hadley had been my go-to person when we were growing up, but I didn't know what kind of reception I'd get now. I thought about calling her now, but didn't want to deal with Jim if he answered the phone. Todd had asked that I wait until he told his children. Working at the society would take my mind off my personal issues.

About an hour later, I pulled into the parking lot of the historical society. Kevin Angetti was on the walkway. The museum wasn't open; there was no reason for him to be here. His family had only one car, so he was dropped off before his cousin drove to work at the gas station. If I wanted to be alone, I would need to drive him into town. As I was contemplating how to politely do that, Irene Phelps, the historical society's administrator, drove into the lot. She sat in her car, pulled out a compact, and proceeded to check her makeup and hair.

Irene got out of the car. "I talked to Grace's family last night and they wanted to—" She stopped when her high heels hit a patch of mud and she fell forward. She caught herself before she landed and straightened out. Not a hair out of place, and her makeup still looked perfect. She continued as if the mud were a mere inconvenience. "Grace's family wants to have the memorial service here at the historical society, in the church. I told them that it wasn't a problem, but I needed to check on the church and figure out when it could take place."

We walked up to the door and Kevin followed us. Irene wrangled with the door and disabled the alarm. "I asked Kevin to come this morning, to move the podium upstairs and any other heavy lifting we might need for the service. Doesn't look too bad, luckily," said Irene as we went inside. "The cleaners will deal with the dust and clean the rugs."

"Have you called them?" I asked.

Irene assured me, in her efficient way, that she had and they could come on Friday. If we got everything else arranged today, the memorial could be next week. Some of the pictures and boxes had fallen off the shelves during the winter. Irene and I went through them and put them back in place. Kevin went downstairs to find the podium and tables we needed for the service. I asked Irene about the barn and she said that the locksmith was due today to put new locks on. The alarm company was coming tomorrow to update the system.

Church bells rang out. Irene's phone—she was the wife of a minister. "Sorry, got to get this." She walked down the staircase. I could hear her murmuring but couldn't make out the words.

I took a slow walk around the sanctuary. Mice were not the only creatures that wanted to spend the winter in the church. Sometimes larger animals got in, but I found no signs of forced entry or wildlife damage. Guess the person living in the barn didn't want to enter the church or the offices where people worked.

Irene came back into the sanctuary. "Grace is going to be buried tomorrow," she said. "It'll be a private matter, just the family. Then we'll have the public memorial, here, a week from Sunday. That gives us time to clean up and get things ready." She leaned down, picked up a hymnal on the floor, and replaced it on the back table. "Shouldn't we do something for the family?"

Irene knew what to do in difficult circumstances. She always had time to talk. I wanted to spill everything, about the baby and my nightmares about Grace, but I'd promised Todd. Maybe later.

"I've ordered flowers for the family. Do you think we need to do something for the burial?" I set down my water bottle. "And I made a casserole to take to the house." I hadn't baked it yet, but I did have good intentions.

"I planned to go see the family tomorrow morning, about eleven," said Irene. "Before the burial—that's in the afternoon. Do you want to come with me?"

I wanted to ask the family some questions, but hadn't figured out how to do it. Talking about Grace would be the natural thing to do. Tagging along with Irene, I'd just be another visitor offering condolences. "Sounds good, I can do it then." And it gave me a day to bake the casserole.

"Can I get some help down here?" Kevin's voice came up the stairwell.

"Probably needs help getting the podium and the table up the stairs," said Irene. "I'll help him; I don't want you lifting heavy things in your condition." Irene went down the stairs. This reminded me, once again, that too many people knew about my pregnancy. I hoped that Todd told Brian and Dierdre before they heard it from someone else.

Well, while I was waiting, I could check the rest of the sanctuary. The red cushions on the pews showed signs of wear. Not that the original congregants would have had cushions, but it was necessary for contemporary bottoms. Our mice had gnawed a hole in one of the cushions and stolen some of its stuffing, probably to build a nest. Only one other one had a visible hole. I had both cushions in my arms when Irene and Kevin returned with the lectern.

"What are you doing with those?" asked Kevin. "Don't they belong on the seats?"

"Holes." I showed him. "Probably from mice. They'll need to be mended."

"I can do that," said Irene.

I'd counted on that as Irene was the local seamstress also. I sewed almost as badly as I cooked. We moved the furniture into place, checked the exhibits, and cleaned the more delicate pieces. Irene called to confirm the professional cleaners would come on Friday. We were putting the cushions in her car when the locksmith arrived. She said that she had it under control and I needed to eat something before my afternoon interview.

I noticed a paper stuck under the wipers on my car. When I got it out, I saw printing on it in block letters: *Your going to be sorry*. I don't accept threats from people who are not even literate, so I crumpled it up and threw it on the floor of the car.

By the time we finished and Irene and Kevin left, it was twelve thirty. I had just enough time to gulp down a peanut butter and jelly sandwich before the troopers arrived. So much for time to do research.

CHAPTER ELEVEN

Troopers Gray and Bachelor arrived for our meeting ten minutes early, just as I was washing the peanut butter off my hands. Gray came down the stairs and into the conference room first, followed by Bachelor, holding the file box. I asked them to wait a minute and I went into the archive room to get my own documents. We all sat down at the table and they indicated they didn't need water or anything to drink. I pushed the images of Grace out of my mind, and made the first comment.

"I think Grace's death is related to the creation of the Quabbin Reservoir. All the documents you found are eighty to a hundred years old."

Gray folded her hands on the table. She reminded me of my fourth-grade teacher, also given to lecturing me about why I was wrong. "In most cases, we find the reason for murder is a contemporary hatred, or revenge, or a love triangle. That's what we're looking for."

"But the reason Grace was removing items from the museum, if she did it at all, was because of what happened to her grandmother. And her great-aunt's letter was found under her body."

"We have no proof that Grace was removing items from the museum. You yourself said that you were just starting a discussion with her about what was missing."

Gray put her hands flat on the table, but she still reminded me of my fourth-grade teacher.

"But who else would want her dead? She was killed with the Enfield town seal; doesn't that show her connection to the museum? Someone came to the museum specifically to kill her." Couldn't these troopers see what was right in front of them?

"She was seen arguing with Kevin Angetti just days before the murder," said Bachelor. "They seem to have some anger between them, and Kevin has a record."

"Kevin's record is for painting graffiti on the train station and an open container violation," I said. "And he and Grace argue all the time."

"How do you know about Kevin's record?" Bachelor leaned closer to me. "And what did he and Grace argue about?"

"We run record checks on all our employees. It's good business. We decided to give Kevin a chance and we haven't been disappointed." I chose not to answer the second question.

"And Kevin has worked here four years? About the same time as you?" Bachelor made a scribble in his notebook. "Did you know him before he worked here?"

"Yeah, I've known Kevin since I was a teenager. His family sold me my first car when I was seventeen." The car broke down on a weekly basis, but they didn't need to know that.

Trooper Gray reentered the conversation. "What did Grace and Kevin argue about?"

"Business," I said. "Only business."

They both stared at me.

"Grace wanted the museum to continue to be a repository of artifacts from the creation of the Quabbin." I knew these arguments cold, and I could see the value of both sides. "Kevin wanted to use social media and modern lighting and special effects to enhance the experience and bring in younger patrons. They often got quite loud. But they never came to blows and nobody got killed because of those differences."

"You'd be surprised why people kill," said Gray. "Maybe an argument got out of hand. Maybe the town seal was an instrument of convenience."

My mind flashed to the note on my car. "Maybe someone still wants to steal from the museum," I said. "I found a note on my car."

"What did it say?" asked Bachelor. "And where is the note now?"

I felt some embarrassment to say that I'd crumpled it up and thrown it into my car. Bachelor asked for my car keys and went to retrieve it.

"Why didn't you tell us about the note sooner?" asked Gray.

"I was more angry than afraid," I said. "Just threw it away."

Bachelor returned with the note in an evidence bag. Gray put it into her file box. "Now, what about the documents you wanted to talk about?" Guess the discussion about the note on the car was over.

I laid out the documents I'd just taken out of the archive room. "Look at these," I said.

"What are they?" asked Gray.

"The green booklet is the Grange schedule for Enfield for 1935 and 1936. The document is the mortgage and sale of Grace's great-grandfather's equipment to the Shaws. These are the documents Grace produced to prove that the ice harvesting equipment belonged to her and that the Shaws stole from her family."

Gray tapped her finger on the table. "Again, we have no proof of that."

"But Grace believed it. Look at the documents. The Baumans, Grace's ancestors, were well known in town and Grace's great-grandfather and his brother were master and overseer of the Grange for years. Then, in 1937, he was forced to sell his ice harvesting business, at a loss, to Edwin Shaw. Shaw's wife, Lillian, was active in the Grange too and may have arranged the sale. Grace was convinced that her family was swindled out of a fortune."

"But what does that have to do with the murder? Surely nobody carries a grudge for that long."

"Grace did." I'm good at pointing out the obvious.

"We are looking for a more recent motive," said Bachelor. "Maybe your job requires that you live in the past, but we are looking for a more contemporary reason for murder. Other than yourself and Kevin, has Grace argued with anyone else in the last few weeks?"

"Kevin and me? Are we your prime suspects? That's ridiculous."

"We don't suspect you," said Gray. "In the hours before you arrived at the museum, we have you at the grocery store, the post office, and the library."

I'd forgotten the errands that had made me late to my appointment with Grace. But obviously the police had been checking. Todd told me that the average person was on video dozens of times a day and it seemed to be true. Then I realized what Gray didn't say. "What about Kevin? He can't be a suspect."

"King Phillip Motors, the auto body shop his family owns, only has cameras on the outside yard." Bachelor flipped through his notebook. "Yup, one camera over the front door and one in the salvage yard. Rather strange for a company when the money is kept inside. But Kevin doesn't appear on video there or anywhere else. Only people who saw him at work are related to him. Most of them have criminal records of their own."

This can't be right. I went over my story of finding Grace one more time and the troopers asked the same questions they had the last time. I tried to stress Grace's obsession with the past and the importance of what happened to her family. They weren't buying it.

By the time we finished, I was exhausted. But I needed to do more research on my own, to learn more about the history of the families. I went downstairs and unlocked the archive room. I'd just sat down when I heard footsteps on the stairs. Were the police coming back to ask more questions? It didn't sound like the boots of the state troopers.

ENFIELD GRANGE
SCHEDULE FOR 1935-1936

Officers for September 1935 to August 1936
Master:	Francis S. Bauman
Overseer:	William A. Bauman
Steward:	Edwin P. Mitchell
Chaplain:	Mrs. Edwin (Lillian) Shaw
Treasurer:	Walter P. Farnum
Secretary:	Keith Knight

Programs for 1935-1936
September 1935:	Installation and Feast
October 1935:	Lecture #1
November 1935:	Discussion: What makes a more competent cattle inspector, a practical farmer or a graduate veterinarian?
December 1935:	Christmas Pageant
January 1936:	Lecture #2
February 1936:	Discussion: Which is the better policy, for a farmer to buy or raise his own dairy cattle?
March 1936:	St. Patrick's Day dance, with a new way to find your partner
April 1936:	Installation of New Degrees
May 1936:	Neighbors Night
June 1936:	Lecture #3
July 1936:	Independence Celebration and preparations for Grange Fair in August
August 1936:	Final preparations for Grange Fair

CHAPTER TWELVE

"Emma? You down here?"

I let out a breath I didn't know I was holding. It was just Irene.

"In here, Irene. Just doing some research." I took another deep breath. "I guess I'm just jumpy, since the murder."

"The locksmith has put new, more secure locks on the barn, so that is less of a worry." I'm glad that Irene didn't say that it was not a worry. It still bothered me.

Irene looked at the papers on the table. "Can I help?"

Irene had only worked for the society for a few weeks. She was good at organization—she was administrative coordinator after all—but the archive room was still a mystery to her. She looked around.

"Can't believe you know where everything is in this room." Irene closed the door behind her. "What are you looking for?"

"History on Grace and her family. They lived in the valley for over a hundred years before her family was forced out of Enfield. In the twentieth century, they gained some wealth." I walked back to the box containing old Patrons of Husbandry pamphlets and pulled it off the shelf. "What are you still doing here? I thought you left a few hours ago."

"I did, but I came back." Irene looked around the room. "I mean, I went to the country store for lunch, then came back to check on you. You know, after you talked to the cops again."

"That's sweet, but I'm fine."

"I can see that," said Irene. "I mean, I thought you might be upset. And I want to help with the research."

I gave her the box I was holding. "You can go through this box for any mention of the Bauman family. Francis and William were brothers. Francis had three daughters: Rachel, Alma, and Elizabeth. Alma died young and Elizabeth was a dozen years younger than her sisters. Elizabeth is now Betsy Adams."

Irene looked down at the box. "What were the Patrons of Husbandry?"

"Sit down, I'll give you a short history lesson."

Irene and I sat in the straight-back chairs. I put my feet up on a third chair. "The Patrons of Husbandry are also known as the Grange. After the Civil War, farmers banded together to get better prices for their produce and to get the railroads to lower their tariffs. Almost every adult in the valley had something to do with the Grange."

"Women too? Or just men?"

"Women too," I said. "That was a strength of the Grange. Since its founding, a certain number of positions and members had to be female." I hesitated before giving her the next piece of information, but if I'm going to talk about the pluses, I also need to include the minuses. "On the down side, especially in the South, the Granges were a front for the Ku Klux Klan. Though that didn't seem to be an issue in Swift River."

"How would you know? It's not like they'd advertise it," Irene pointed out.

"True," I said. "And for a time, William and Francis Bauman were master and overseer of the local Grange."

"Master and overseer. That doesn't sound suspicious."

I had to get Irene off this topic. I didn't want to relive the shadowy past; I wanted to learn more about the Bauman family. "The Grange worked for the farmers in the valley. It was a sign of respect and their standing in the community that the Bauman brothers rose to the most important positions."

"But Grace was always complaining about losing her family's legacy," said Irene. "Doesn't sound much like respect to me."

I knew this part without looking it up. "William Bauman's daughter, Alma, drowned, and he blamed himself. He was an ice harvester."

"Ice harvester?" Irene stopped going through the box in front of her. "What's that?"

"Before there were electric refrigerators, they had iceboxes."

"Like the one in the summer kitchen with the zinc lining."

"Exactly. The men harvested ice from the ponds every winter. They cut huge chunks of ice, put them in an ice house near the water, and covered the ice blocks with sawdust. Between the sawdust insulation and the cool water from the pond, the ice lasted into the summer."

"And then the ice man delivered it to houses, and put it in the top of the ice box. The food underneath stayed cold that way." Irene grinned. "I really am trying to learn more about this museum. It seemed like a nice, quiet place to live, with farms and ponds."

"It wasn't all bucolic," I said. "Before the land was sold to the state, there was quite a bit of industry in the valley. The Swift River Box Company, grist mills, and, of course, the hat factories."

"Yes," said Irene. "I remember reading a letter about making hats at home. Was there a factory too?"

"Oh, yes, and it made millions of hats for the world. Even in a time when almost everyone wore a hat, there was a disproportionate number made in Dana. Panama hats, top hats, and ladies' bonnets."

I pulled out one of the oversized archive boxes. "In here, there is a special section on the Swift River Valley; it ran in the *Worcester Telegram and Gazette* in 1905." I pulled out the yellowed pages in their Mylar sleeves.

"Tell me more," said Irene. "I know so little about the valley before the Quabbin. We moved here because it was a protected water and great for hiking. I didn't know about the history."

"Unfortunately, many people don't know about the history. How the land was taken to provide drinking water for Boston. Most people there don't know where their water comes from." I laid the pages of the newspaper out on the table. "I don't like generalizations, but it's a great shortcut. Dana and North Dana, especially near the railroad tracks, were the manufacturing towns. Enfield was the wealthiest town; many people had summer homes or came to the lakes for a break from the city. Greenwich and Prescott were the farming towns. Though farming was tougher in Prescott; it's a rocky raised area, now a peninsula. But the people who lived here loved their towns and didn't want to move. I can recommend some books, if you want more information.

"But, back to the Baumans. William Bauman had no sons so he took his daughters, Rachel and Alma, to help him harvest the ice. Alma fell into the pond and drowned."

"Weren't they young to be harvesting ice?" Irene stared off into space. "It must be awful to lose a child."

"That may be one reason why Bauman felt so guilty. Rachel was sixteen and Alma was just fourteen when she drowned. The third sister, Betsy, was just a toddler. She claims not to remember her sister."

"But Betsy wanted justice." Irene took some documents out of the box in front of her.

"Even Betsy has mellowed with age," I said. "But Grace, her granddaughter, has taken up the fight."

"What fight?"

"After Alma's death, William Bauman fell apart, started drinking. He ignored his farm work and had to sell his ice harvesting business." I pulled an Enfield record book off the shelf; it had a yellow sticky note sticking up between the pages. The book fell open to the marked page. "This was one of the documents that obsessed Grace. It's the mortgage, selling her father's equipment to Edwin Shaw. Says that he didn't pay the going price for the equipment, that Shaw cheated Bauman."

"Grace took back the ice harvesting equipment from the museum?" Irene asked. "What was she going to do with it, try to sell it again?"

I don't know," I said. "I'm not sure she was thinking rationally about it. Hell, I'm not even sure she took it."

"Just a minute." Irene laid one of the Grange pamphlets on the table. "This is the Grange officers for 1935. William Bauman is the overseer and a Mrs. Edwin (Lillian) Shaw is the chaplain. Shaw's wife was a Grange officer too?"

"Not unusual," I said. "Most everybody belonged to the Grange. But Grace thought that Mrs. Shaw might have influenced the sale." I picked up the Enfield record and put it back on the shelf. "Of course, we're talking about events that happened almost a century ago. We have no way of knowing what people were thinking then."

"But we have all this." Irene flapped her hand at the archive room.

"And in here, somewhere, may be the answers to our questions. If we can find them." I pulled out a pad of paper and a pen. "To start, let's make a list of the questions we need to answer."

Irene and I put our heads together and, in about forty minutes, came up with our list:

- *Who killed Grace?*
- *What was Grace doing in the museum hours before our meeting?*

- *Who else was in the museum?*
- *Did Grace take the documents and equipment from the museum?*
- *If so, why did she take the documents and equipment?*
- *How did it tie in with her obsession about her family being cheated out of its heritage?*
- *What does Betsy Adams know about what happened ninety years ago?*
- *What were the details of Alma's death? Was there an investigation?*
- *How was the rest of the family affected by Alma's death? What exactly did it do to William Bauman?*

"That's some list," said Irene. "Where do we start?"

"I'm exhausted," I said. "Between Grace's death, and the troopers, and the questions. Let's start tomorrow morning with Betsy Adams. Maybe she can narrow down the search parameters."

"Is that why you wanted to go to the house with me?" asked Irene. "Not for a condolence call, but to question the family?"

I was too tired to lie. "I had mixed motives," I said. "I do care about the family and I will bring a casserole." Still had to make it, though. "But I thought I might get Betsy to talk about Grace and her family. It may come up naturally in conversation."

"I figured," Irene said, taking her car keys out of her purse. "I'll pick you up around ten thirty, here at the museum."

Miss Rachel Alice Bauman
43 Turnpike Road
Enfield, Massachusetts

February 23, 1937
Dear Louisa:

I have terrible, terrible news for you. My sister, Alma, is dead. Mama cries all the time and Papa blames himself for her death. I don't know whether I can stand to stay in this house much longer. The only thing that keeps me here is my little sister, Betsy. She is so young, just three years old, and she needs someone to care for her. At the present time, I'm the only one who attends to her needs.

Alma fell through the ice on the pond and drowned. Or she froze to death. I heard the men in the parlor discussing how she died, as if that is the most important thing about her passing. Alma has been laid out in the parlor for three days now and each night the neighborhood men come and drink with Papa next to the coffin. I think one of the men has a still under the barn, for no alcohol is for sale.

Today, she will be taken to the cemetery and put into the town vault. We will bury her in the spring, after the ground thaws. Though I'm reluctant to say it, I'm glad she's leaving this house. Maybe after she is gone, Mama and Papa won't have a constant reminder and things may move forward. We won't forget, but maybe we can move past the grief.

Papa had Alma and I go with him to harvest the ice on the pond. Now that the factories have closed, we have little income, so Papa rented the equipment back from Mr. Shaw. He was upset that he had to rent his own equipment, but Mr.

Shaw gave him a fair price. Papa decided that Alma and I would help him with the harvest; Betsy is too young and Mama had to stay with her. It was freezing out on the pond and I stole one of the horse blankets to wrap myself in when I was not working. Standing by the horses also helped, as their heat made me warmer. Papa cut a hole for the ice harvesting and cut a conduit to the horses, so that we could float the ice out of the pond. Papa then lifted it onto the wagon.

Alma and I were to take the ice after it was cut from the pond, and guide it to the horses. By lunch, both Alma and I were exhausted and happy to stop and eat the hot soup Mama brought from the house. I was still sitting on the shore when Papa and Alma went out to determine where the next cutting would take place. I heard a shout and saw Alma slip off the ice and into the water. Papa tried to grab her, but he could not get to her. He chopped the ice and, after what seemed like an eternity, was able to pull her from the pond. The horses took her to the house. Papa laid her on the ice during the trip and then brought her into the house. Mama cried when she saw Alma, all cold and blue, but Papa said some people survive the cold water, because their body shuts down.

Papa insisted that we lay Alma by the fire and allow her body to thaw and, perhaps, for her to revive. We waited several hours and she remained silent. It was heartbreaking to watch Mama gain hope as Alma's body got warmer and allow herself to be reassured by Papa. When it became clear that Alma was gone, both of them cried. I have never seen Papa cry before, even when Grammom passed.

Louisa, I am sorry to burden you with my melancholy, but I needed to say this to someone and my family is devastated and not paying much attention to Betsy and me.

Please come visit, if you can do so, as I would like to see your face again and wander about the valley with you. Papa hopes to keep Alma's passing out of the local papers, so I will write to you when I know more about a service in the spring.

Pray for me and my family.
Rachel

WORCESTER TELEGRAM AND GAZETTE

WORCESTER WEST: SWIFT RIVER VALLEY　　　　APRIL 1, 1905

OVERVIEW OF SWIFT RIVER VALLEY

Nature has done much for the Swift River Valley, making it one of the most desired places in the state not only for manufacturing purposes and permanent residency, but also as a summer resort. Its romantic and picturesque surroundings, its numerous delightful drives in nature offer unusual inducements to tourists, tired of the dirt and noise of city life.

Greenwich Lake, with its golf course and summer camps, offers a relaxing experience. Anglers can get their limits from the branches of the Swift River and those requiring more strenuous exercise can climb Mount Zion.

There is something for everyone in the Swift River Valley, whether they spend a day or a lifetime.

COLT ARMORY PRESS

The Swift River Gazette does printing, the best work at the lowest prices. All work is done on a Colt's Armory Press, the absolute authority for quality printing. The Colt Armory is a state-of-the-art machine, capable of fulfilling any business needs. Its export protectors ensure that the printed matter goes directly to a drying bin and is not touched or smudged before it is dry. The press uses paper from local trees, and is inspected to ensure that it is free of imperfections and of the highest quality. Inks are carefully selected for vividness and clarity, ensuring each customer is satisfied.

SWIFT RIVER BOX COMPANY

The Swift River Box Company of Dana, Massachusetts serves the world. The building has three portals of ingress and egress for its many employees. The building is wood and its machines are powered by steam. The basement consists of indoor sanitary facilities, for the health and safety of all.

The rooms where the boxes are constructed have high ceilings and tall windows, so that most of the work can be done in natural light. All inventory is inspected and sealed by hand before it goes for retail sale.

MORTGAGE OF PERSONAL PROPERTY

I, Francis S. Bauman of Enfield, Commonwealth of Massachusetts, the receipt whereof is hereby acknowledged by Edwin Shaw, do hereby grant, sell, transfer, and deliver to said Edwin Shaw, the following goods and chattel, namely:

- 2 meat carts
- 2 meat boxes
- 2 express sleighs
- 1 farm wagon
- 1 express wagon
- 1 express harness
- 1 driving harness
- 1 sleigh
- 1 barge
- 1 ice plow
- 1 ice scraper
- 1 set falls with rope
- 1 grapple and rope for ice harvesting
- 3 horse blankets
- 2 horse covers
- 1 Makaska register and safe
- 1 grind stone

To have and hold all the said goods and chattel to said Edwin Shaw and his executors, administrators, and assigns to their use and behold forever. And I hereby state to the grantee that I am the lawful owner of the said goods and chattels; that they are free from all encumbrances, that I have good right to sell the same aforementioned and that I will warrant and defend the same against all lawful claims and demands of all persons. Provided nevertheless that if I, or any executors, administrators, or assigns, shall be paid the sum of three hundred dollars ($300) with interest as stated in my note of even date signed by me and until such payment shall keep the said goods and chattels insured against fire in a sum not less than one hundred dollars ($100) for the benefit of the grantee and his executors, administrators, and assigns, in such form and in such insurance companies as they shall approve, I shall not waste or destroy the said goods and chattels, nor suffer them or any part thereof, to be attached, and shall not, except with the consent in writing of the grantee or his representative, attempt to sell or to remove from buildings of grantee the same or any part thereof, or this deed, as also the foresaid note, shall be void. But upon any default in the note or any of its parts, the grantee or his representative shall be entitled to retain all sums then secured by this mortgage, whether then or thereafter payable, including all costs, charges, and expense incurred or sustained by them in relation to said property, or to discharge any claims or liens of third persons affecting the same, rendering the surplus, if any, to me or my executors, administrators, or assigns.

  In witness whereof we, the said Francis S. Bauman and Edwin Shaw, set our hands and seals this nineteenth day of January in the Year 1937.

CHAPTER THIRTEEN

I stopped by the museum early the next morning. Not that I had any specific reason, I just wanted to know that things were getting back to normal. As I pulled in, I saw a truck parked in the driveway. "Armand's Curiosities & Collectibles" was painted on the side in Gothic letters, with a phone number underneath it. Standing beside the truck was a large man over sixty years old, no neck, broad shoulders, dressed in faded brown overalls. He looked up when I got out of my car and slammed the door.

I walked toward him. "Can I help you?"

He looked around as if I were talking to someone behind him. His hands formed fists at his sides. I realized I was out in the country, by myself, with a man who looked like he lifted large weights for a living. I stopped.

"I'm Armand." He gestured toward the truck. "I'm looking for Grace. Supposed to meet her here."

"I'm Emma, the archivist. Grace didn't tell me you were coming." Let him think I wasn't here alone. I'd tell him about Grace later.

"We meet every week about this time," he said. "Have coffee, talk about things."

"What things?'

He pushed his hand through his hair. The salt-and-pepper military cut didn't move. "I'd like to talk to Grace."

"What do you want?" I pulled out my phone, and kept it, visible, in my hand. Let him think I might call the cops.

"Grace and I were going to do some business. She said she had some things she wanted me to see."

"Things from the museum?"

He looked back toward the truck. "She collected things on her own. Said the museum was trying to get rid of some duplicate stuff. I pay good prices."

Grace did buy and sell curiosities and collectibles but, as far as I knew, most of her sales were on the internet, not in person. But I was certain that the museum hadn't authorized the sale of any items for over a year. I was wondering what to do when there was a crash from the carriage shed.

"What the hell was that?" I was asking the question as I hurried to the closed door.

It slid open easily. I stepped into the carriage shed and was nose-to-nose with the Dana fire truck. I couldn't see anything in the darkened interior of the shed. Too late, I realized I was alone with an unknown man in a dark enclosed space. I'd had years of moving around the historical society without worries. This new suspicion of everyone made me uncomfortable. I heard footsteps behind me and turned to see Armand in the doorway. Without hesitation, he went to the light switches and flipped them on.

"Hey, Dad, look what I found." The voice came from behind the firetruck.

Armand brushed past me and turned to the right.

"Now I am calling the cops." I started pressing buttons on the phone still in my hand.

Armand's hand came over mine. He was fast, and quiet. "Don't do that."

He took my arm and guided me around the truck. Up against the back wall stood a young man with the long legs and lanky look of adolescence. His blond hair hung in his eyes and he wore a hooded sweatshirt that said "Mahar Senators," with a logo that looked more like a centurion. In his arms was a stack of pictures and books. When he saw me, he slid the entire pile onto the shelf behind him.

"What the hell are you doing?" I don't often swear, but this seemed like the right occasion. I punched 911 into my phone.

"This is my son, Jesse," Armand said.

"911, what is your emergency?" I put the phone on speaker so both Jesse and Armand could hear. "This is Emma Wetherby at the Swift River Historical Society in New Salem, Massachusetts." I swallowed hard, remembering making the same phone call, with the same words about Grace. I prayed that this situation would have a better outcome. "There are two men in the museum. I don't know who they are and they are not authorized to be here." I looked at Armand. "One of them tried to prevent me from calling you."

"This is so unnecessary," said Armand.

"Are they there with you now?" asked the dispatcher.

"Yes, it's Armand from Armand's Curiosities and Collectibles and another person. They aren't supposed to be here and I want them gone." I wished I'd thought to get the license plate number of the truck.

"I'm sending someone now," said the dispatcher. "Please stay on the line."

Armand came over to me, took the phone, and disconnected the call. "That was not a good idea. We're here to meet Grace, nothing else."

I walked over to the pile of items Jesse put on the shelf. He had left the area while his father and I were on the call. Two miniature pictures of ice harvesting (one a reproduction) and three schoolbooks from the 1920s.

"What was that kid doing with these items?" I asked. "And how did he get into the shed?"

Armand came over to stand by me. "He was just looking at them," he said. "Jesse's my son." As if that explained everything.

"In the dark?" I shook my head. "The books belong in the schoolroom and the pictures were on the wall near the door. Both on the other side of the shed."

"Maybe he brought them to the window to see them better." Armand picked up the items and took them over toward the door.

"How did you know where the light switches were?" I asked. "You went directly to them."

"Been here before." He put the books into the schoolroom. "Where do the pictures go?"

I walked over and took them from him. "Not so fast. How did your son get in here? And how do you two get off making yourselves at home?" I felt bolder, now I knew somebody was on the way here.

"The door was open," said Armand. "And I told you, we meet Grace here on a regular basis."

"What about the alarm? Why didn't that go off when you came in here?" Damn my problems with the alarm system.

"Don't know anything about the alarm." Armand stepped outside the shed. "Jesse. Jesse, where the hell are you?" He started toward the house.

Jesse appeared at the steps. "Dad, come here. You need to see this."

Armand hurried toward the house and I scurried close behind. We reached Jesse, who was pointing at the yellow-and-black crime scene tape, still a barricade to the back door.

Armand stopped. "Something stolen from here?" he asked.

"Maybe it was the—" Jesse stopped mid-sentence when Armand waved his hand.

"Maybe it's what?" Now I was more confused than ever. "You'll have to explain to the police when they get here."

Armand turned toward me. "What was stolen?" he asked.

I let out a sigh of relief. At least his thoughts had gone to robbery, or larceny, not murder. Or else he was a very good liar. Either way, I might as well tell him.

"Nothing was stolen," I said. "Grace was murdered. Here."

"Murdered?" asked Jesse. "How did that happen?"

"She was hit over the head. In the Enfield Room. State police were here most of the day."

Armand grabbed Jesse by the arm. "Come on, we're getting out of here." He led Jesse across the lawn, and they got in the truck and drove away. I got the "2" and the "N" of the plate, but the rest was just a blur.

I went to check the barn. The new lock was in place and the door didn't move when I tried to open it. The alarm was armed and working in the Whitaker-Clary House. The church was locked.

I looked down at the phone in my hand and did a search for "Armand's Curiosities and Collectibles." It had a website that proclaimed they had been in business for fifteen years. Lots of four- and five-star reviews. Some pictures of Texaco signs and ancient wringer washers. Looked like the website was homemade.

Todd entered the parking lot. I went over to the cruiser and gave him the short version of what happened. Irene pulled into the parking lot as I was talking to Todd. He told me to stay with Irene until he got things straightened out; then took off down the road in the direction the truck had gone.

Irene came over to stand by me. "Are you okay? Did he hurt you?"

"No," I said. "I'm just not used to being on my guard at the museum. I think of it as a place of refuge."

"Refuge from what?" Irene led me over to the church and we sat down in a back pew. "What are you worried about?"

I went through the shortened version of my worries. Irene listened intently and nodded at all the right places.

"I'm worried about this baby, whether he'll be healthy," I said, nearing the end of my rant. "And Todd doesn't seem interested in marriage, but I think parents should be committed to each other."

"Do you think he's committed to you?"

Put that bluntly, Irene made me think. "He's had a bad marriage and he raised Carol's son, and this baby wasn't planned. I've always wanted to be a mother, but he seems like he's already moved past that stage."

"I think parents should be committed to each other, too," said Irene. "But maybe you should consider whether you've already put too much into this relationship."

She stopped speaking after that statement. We sat in silence until Todd returned to say that he couldn't find Armand or the truck. Irene and I left to visit with Betsy Adams and Gretchen Connelly.

CHAPTER FOURTEEN

Irene and I arrived at the Connelly home at five after eleven later that morning. Any delay was my fault, as I was still rattled about my confrontation with Armand and his son. And I hate it when people get to my house early, while I'm still trying to set up and get the last-minute details right. Of course, a condolence call is different, but it's not like the Connelly family didn't have other things to do. Irene carried a fruit basket, almost too big for her arms, and I had the casserole with me. Chicken and broccoli in my special cream sauce. I'm not much of a cook, but it's one dish that works for potlucks, church events, and funerals. The house was a blue ranch house that needed painting and repairs to the porch. Someone had attempted to liven up the place with red begonias in the window boxes and pansies in urns on the front porch. It was still April and cold at night; I wondered who took the boxes in at night and then brought them out in the morning.

Gretchen Connelly, Grace's mother, answered the door. She was a formidable woman, almost six feet tall, with broad shoulders. I'd heard that she almost made the Olympic swim team fifty years ago. Today, her eyes were red and she wore a loose white shirt over jeans.

Accompanying her were three dogs. They looked like labradoodles, one full size and two toys. Todd and I had considered that breed when we were looking for dogs. Might consider it again; labradoodles were known for not shedding, unlike our hairball, Barney. I had just finished that thought when the largest dog took off, out the door and towards the road.

Without thinking, I took off after the dog. It didn't seem at all concerned and started trotting down the middle of the road. I hurried to keep up. This was a rural road, not much traffic, but, for that same reason, people tended to drive too fast, not expecting to meet anyone else. Someone could come around the corner, not see the wayward pet, and hit the animal.

The dog stopped and walked into the woods at the side of the road. It took me a few seconds to get to the spot where it had disappeared. I couldn't keep running; I needed another strategy. I reached into my pocket and found a few crackers. Seemed I was always stuffing crackers into my pockets to counteract the morning sickness. I held them out, toward the dog. Not much of a treat, but I was counting on its curiosity to do the rest. It sniffed, tentatively, and then took the food from my hand. I grabbed it by the collar and walked it back to the house.

"Oh, thank goodness, you found her," Gretchen said. She was standing in the yard and she must have had the same idea I had, because she held a can of dog treats. When we got close enough, she grabbed the collar and marched the dog into the house. "Bad dog. You know you're not supposed to do that."

Gretchen looked at me. "She's usually very well behaved. I guess she's confused about Grace being gone. Please come in. Mother and I have just finished breakfast."

I followed her into the house. "Do you mind the dogs?" she asked. "I can put them in the back if it's a problem. Though you seem to handle them well."

I looked at Irene, who shook her head. "Not a problem," I said. "The big dog and I have become well acquainted."

"That's Prescott," said Gretchen. "The little ones are Dana and Enfield."

Alone at the dining room table was an older version of Grace. She had the same bobbed hair and hazel eyes. Her hair was grayer than Grace's and needed a comb run through it. She sat ramrod straight, though she had to be over ninety years old, and took a sip from a mug in front of her. "The dogs belonged to Grace," said the older women, who had to be Betsy Adams. "They're a constant reminder of her, for good and bad."

"Prescott is misbehaving," said Gretchen to the older woman. She explained that I had run after her and coaxed her back to the house. To Irene and me, she issued an invitation to sit down.

"I can see the visitors," said the older woman. "Excuse me if I don't get up, my hip is bothering me."

"No problem, Mrs. Adams."

"Call me Betsy." The old woman took another sip. "Do you want coffee? Or something stronger?"

"Coffee would be lovely." Irene sat down at the table and I sat next to her. Gretchen went into the kitchen.

"I'm so sorry about the death of your granddaughter," I said. The full-size dog came over and put his head on my lap.

"Heard you were the one who found her," Betsy said. "Why was she at the historical society that time of day anyway?"

I didn't have to answer the question right away, as Gretchen returned with coffee, cream, and sugar on a silver tray. She put it next to the fruit basket and the casserole, already on the table.

"Our condolences," said Irene. "It's so sad about Grace. She was a fixture at the historical society."

"Thank you," said Gretchen. "Would you like something with your coffee? We have so much food, and now this lovely fruit basket." She picked up the casserole. "I'll just put this in the kitchen. Do you want anything else?"

Both Irene and I shook our heads and Gretchen left the room again.

"So, why was my granddaughter at the society on a day that she wasn't scheduled to work?" It appeared that Betsy wasn't going to give up on her question.

"Grace and I had a meeting," I said. "About some events going on at the historical society."

"You mean the missing equipment and pictures." Betsy set down her coffee cup and moved it to the side of the table. "You think my granddaughter had something to do with the missing things."

"Not really." I don't think I even convinced myself. "I'm talking to everyone about the missing items. Maybe the society needs a better security system."

"You mean better than the same numbers for all the alarm codes?" asked Gretchen, walking back into the room.

"How did you know that?" I stared at her.

"It's on the card, on the lanyard with the keys." Gretchen gestured toward the kitchen. "She left it in the basket by the door, the morning she left."

Gretchen got quiet and rubbed her eyes. Like she just realized, one more time, that Grace was not coming home.

"Wait a minute." This from Irene. "If she didn't take the keys, how did she get into the historical society that morning?"

"The killer let her in," said Gretchen. "Or at least, that's what the trooper thought."

"You mean Trooper Bachelor?" I asked.

"Don't think that was the name." Betsy put her coffee cup back in front of Gretchen. "I need more coffee."

Gretchen got up to get the pot, returned, and poured. "Short woman, dark skin."

"Trooper Gray?" I asked. "She was here?"

"Just about accused Grace of stealing from the society. Like Grace meant to get herself killed." Betsy took a sip of coffee. "You need to make another pot, Gretchen. This coffee's been sitting around too long."

Gretchen stood up.

"You don't need to make another pot," I said. "Just sit down and talk to us. What evidence did the trooper have that Grace was the thief?"

"Grace wasn't a thief," said Irene. "She was a lovely woman."

Bang. Bang. Bang. Someone was at the front door.

Gretchen got up and pushed aside the curtain on the window beside the door. "It's the church ladies," she said. "No matter how many times I tell them that the doorbell works, they still pound on the door."

"I don't want to talk to them." Betsy picked up her cup, put it in the sink, and left the room. The dogs followed at her heels and Betsy shut the door to a back room, with herself and the dogs inside. Gretchen made a face at her mother's retreating back. Then she opened the front door.

Three church ladies, complete with flowered dresses and brimmed hats, entered the house. They introduced themselves as Eudora, Debra, and Catherine, but it took me a while to tell them apart. Eudora had a red hat with a flower on it, Catherine had a wide black belt around her white, black, and orange dress, and Debra was hatless, but wore a green and pink scarf. They brought more food, went directly to the kitchen, and rearranged the refrigerator to make sure that everything fit. We watched from the dining room.

Gretchen stood in the middle of the kitchen, letting the women swarm around her. Catherine put her hands on her shoulders and suggested that Gretchen needed to make more coffee. Gretchen dumped out the coffee remaining in the pot, rinsed it out, and started another pot.

"Maybe it's time for us to leave." I made a show of checking my watch, then realized I hadn't worn one today. "So you can talk to your new visitors."

"Oh, please stay." Gretchen's mouth flattened to a straight line and, looking directly at me, she rolled her eyes.

"We could stay a few more minutes," said Irene, retaking her place at the table.

"Besides, we have some news to share with you," said the lady with the red hat. Yes, Eudora was her name. "The police may be making an arrest."

"How do you know that?" I asked.

Eudora ran her hands down the front of her dress. "My grandson is in the district attorney's office."

That didn't really answer my question, but I let it go. And I wanted to hear what she thought she knew. We all sat down at the table again. No sign of Betsy.

"Dear, how are you doing?" Catherine reached across the table to take Gretchen's hand. "And how about your mother? Where is she? She hasn't been to church recently."

"My mother is upset and not up to seeing people." Gretchen was a very good liar. I almost believed her. "We're trying to take care of ourselves, to get through this trying time."

"I know, it's weighing on all of us, that there may be someone out there who wants to do us in," said Debra. "Especially those of us connected to the historical society."

I'd never seen Debra at the historical society, and I was there several times, every week. She showed no sign of recognizing me, either. I wondered what her connection was.

"If it's any comfort," said Eudora, "they may be close to making an arrest."

We all looked at her. This was, most likely, the response Eudora hoped to get, as she nodded her head and looked around the room. And it was the second time she'd mentioned it.

"An arrest?" asked Irene.

Yes," said Eudora. "One of the docents, if you can believe it. Kevin Angetti, the young man that's always skulking around there. Took my car to his family's place for service once. Hasn't run right since then."

"I don't believe that Kevin did it," I said.

Almost at the same time, Irene stated, "Kevin doesn't skulk."

Eudora turned to look at us. "I recognize you two now." She pointed her finger at me. "You're the archivist at the historical society. The one from Boston." She made "Boston" sound like an insult.

I wanted to tell her that I only went to university in Boston, but decided that wasn't the relevant issue. "I've been the archivist for four years, and I live in New Salem."

"With the police chief." This from Debra, who adjusted her scarf. "I don't think we should be discussing this situation in front of you. Todd Mitchell's been removed from the investigation."

"Todd was removed from the investigation because I found Grace." My eyes started to tear up as the scene in the Enfield Room came back to me. "I tried to revive her and I couldn't. She was cold and it was horrible and Todd being removed from the case isn't his fault." I picked up my purse and rummaged around for the tissues I kept there. Where the hell were they?

Gretchen placed a box of tissues in front of me. I took a handful, wiped my eyes and blew my nose. Take that, church ladies.

Eudora stood up. "We may have said too much." She picked up her purse from the floor where she had placed it. "I think we need to leave."

The other ladies stood and with a flurry of touches on the arm and "Let me know if there's anything I can do," and left.

I looked at Irene and Gretchen. "That was strange," I said.

Betsy came back into the room, without the dogs, holding several pieces of plastic in her hands. "Thank goodness they left," she said. "Kevin had nothing to do with the murder of my granddaughter."

"How do you know that?" I asked.

"Because of this." She put the stack in her hands on the table. It was a series of plastic sleeves, with old, fragile paper inside. "Be careful, these are originals."

"Originals of what?" I asked. I picked up one of the sleeves.

"Originals that will prove why Grace was murdered." Betsy crossed her arms and stared at me.

I sat down and looked over all the documents. It took me several minutes, but nobody said anything while I took my time. They were additional letters between Louisa and Rachel, letters I had never seen before. "Where did you get these?"

"Had them for years," said Betsy. "Didn't think they were anybody's business but ours. But now Grace is dead."

I came to the bottom of the stack and the original eminent domain document, indicating that the state was taking the Bauman farm and evicting Betsy and her family. "Why show them to me now?"

"Because you tried to help Grace." Betsy laid the documents out in a row in front of her. "Unlike those cows who just want to gossip about the museum. And, though you didn't know anything about us, you went after Prescott. You must be a good person, to help others and like dogs."

"What is Debra's connection to the museum?" I asked. "She acted like she was involved, but I've never seen her there or at any meeting."

"Her husband was quite a bit older than her," said Gretchen. "He donated artifacts, and some money, twenty or thirty years ago. She's been using that to establish her credentials ever since. Even though she's from North Carolina."

Ah, yes, the New England belief that your family had to be here for at least three generations before you were a native. Sometimes expressed by my father as "Just because the cat has kittens in the oven, don't make them biscuits."

"Grace cared about our history," Gretchen continued. "She and Betsy would sit at the table after supper and talk about life in the Quabbin and how to preserve the oral and written records. She was much more fanatic about it than I ever was."

"That's what I told the troopers," I said. "They need to look into the past to solve this murder." I pulled out my phone. "Can I take pictures of these documents? I plan to go back to the historical society to do some more research today and I'd like to use these letters."

"No problem." Betsy gathered the sleeves and pushed them towards me. I started snapping pictures.

"Could you use some help with your research?" This from Irene. I'd forgotten she was still here. Hope this isn't the beginning of "pregnancy brain"; my mother said it affects short-term memory first.

"I'm always open to help," I said.

Gretchen insisted on giving us sandwiches and fruit from the piles of food in the house. We thanked her and left.

Miss Louisa Ames
Pelham, Massachusetts

October 22, 1936
Dear Rachel,

Thank you so much for your letter. Please accept my apologies for failure to return the correspondence, but my family has been settling into the new farm in Pelham. We arrived late in the season, so planting was delayed. The money Father received from the Enfield home paid for our new home and seeds for planting, but I miss the orchards and the dairy cattle. We are planting corn and potatoes, much as the Indians did years ago. These crops can sustain us through the winter. The soil in this area is so much richer than that in the Swift River Valley; Father says that things practically grow themselves. It's due to the Connecticut River in our back yard. It overflows in the spring and deposits new, rich soil every year.

I'm sorry to hear the hat factory closed. I still have the bonnet my mother bought for me on my sixteenth birthday; I surmise I will never get another like it. I will need to buy a new bonnet to wear to the wedding if you and Albert get married.

Speaking of marriage, I have a beau. His name is Stephen Aldred and his family owns the farm across the way. He is tall, and handsome, and he thinks I need him to take care of me. I don't need him as much as he thinks I do, but sometimes it is nice to pretend. We are talking of getting married in the spring and I want you to be here for the big event. You can stay with my family and we can talk about life in the valley. By the spring, the valley may be just a memory. My father went to Boston, to one of the public meetings, and the Commission wants to disincorporate all the towns within the year. Father actually saw Governor Curley, and he said he was loud and obnoxious. He is accusing his money men of embezzling money, when everyone knows that Curley is spending it on his friends. Father says that Curley will be a one-term governor.

Father says that, if the valley towns are disincorporated, there are plans for a Farewell Ball, with food and music and dancing. Our family intends to be there and I am looking forward to seeing you in person and talking about our plans. The event will be melancholy, with everyone saying goodbye, but I am looking forward to seeing old friends.

I must end this letter, as there is someone outside who wishes to purchase corn and cattle feed. Now that Father and the boys are in the field, and Mother is active in the local Grange, I am in charge of running the farm stand. I am getting quite talented at bargaining.

Yours truly,
Louisa

Miss Rachel Alice Bauman
43 Turnpike Road
Enfield, Massachusetts

January 12, 1937
Dear Louisa,

    Times are hard in the Swift River Valley, and I am happy that your family has re-established itself in Pelham and that you are doing well. Our family has found it difficult to sustain ourselves after the closing of the hat factory. Papa attempted to harvest ice this winter, but getting sufficient blocks was difficult, as many ponds had logs floating in them after the clearing operations in the valley. All the trees are to be cut so that they will not absorb water when the valley is flooded. Papa was forced to sell his ice harvesting equipment to Mr. Shaw but the amount he received did not make up for the loss of revenue.

    With all the sawing and blasting in the valley, and the installation of pipes four times my height, the cows are not giving milk like in previous years. Millie, my cow I showed at the fair, won a prize for the quality and amount of her milk production. Her production has gone from thirty-four gallons last year to barely twenty this year. The other cows have experienced similar declines in production. Papa is negotiating a price for the farm, so that we can settle elsewhere and continue our agrarian ways.

    The letterhead on this message is no longer accurate. To ease the burden on my family, I have relocated to Athol and taken a position in the Table Shop here. My new address is: Ladies' Dormitory, Athol Table Shop, Athol, Massachusetts.

Please send your letters here, so that we can continue our friendship.

My relationship with Albert has been strained by the move. At first, we could take the Rabbit Run train from Enfield to Athol, as it ran daily. Some people say it's called that because it stops at every tiny town, jumping like a rabbit all along the tracks. Others say it got its name because each stop took so long that you could go out and hunt rabbits before it started again. Either way, though it took some time, we could meet each other on any day we were free. With the coming of the Metropolitan District Commission, the Rabbit Run shut down. Albert and his family, like ours, will be forced to move, and neither of us knows where our families will settle. Albert is encouraging me to marry him, and set up our own household, but I am reluctant to do so amid such uncertainty.

The whistle just blew, calling us all to work. I will post this letter on my way to the factory gate.

With deepest affection,
Rachel

COMMONWEALTH OF MASSACHUSETTS
TREASURER AND RECEIVER-GENERAL

By virtue of the Act of the Great and General Court so assembled in Suffolk County, Commonwealth of Massachusetts, on this twenty-third day of September, 1937.

There is hereby affixed upon the Property of Francis S. Bauman, of Enfield, County of Worcester, Commonwealth of Massachusetts, the sum of seven thousand dollars ($7,000) for a taking by EMINENT DOMAIN OF THE PROPERTY AT 45 TURNPIKE ROAD, ENFIELD, MASSACHUSETTS, consisting altogether of sixty-two (62) acres, more or less, with all encumbrances, buildings, structures, and chattel thereon.

Wherefore, in the observation of an Act of the Great and General Assembly, sitting in Boston, in Suffolk County, and continued by several prorogations and adjournments to this twenty-third day of September, in the year of Our Lord one thousand nine hundred and thirty-seven.

By the Virtue of the Power and Authority therein given, under our Hand and Seal at Boston, this taking is final.

May

CHAPTER FIFTEEN

The memorial service for Grace took place the first Saturday in May. I was afraid the cleaners wouldn't finish in time but Mary, the supervisor, came to me just after noon on Friday to say that they had finished. I went up to check. Not a trace of winter visitors, cobwebs, or other unwanted debris. Mary and her crew had polished the wooden pews until they gleamed. The other buildings were securely locked. I checked.

Grace had been cremated so, on what had been the altar of the church, a white urn sat, with an enlarged picture of her leading a tour of the museum. Her family had insisted on pictures of her and her life, so the back of the room held easels with displays of childhood pictures, adult pictures, and many photographs of her at the museum. The day was unseasonably warm for May. The plan was for an informal calling hour from two to three, ending with a service.

I stood in the back of the room, leaning against the wall. I didn't have a formal part in the service; the board of directors had arranged the speakers and Gretchen had insisted on the family pastor officiating. My job was to make sure things ran smoothly and that everyone knew where to stand. The family, pitifully small at just

Gretchen and Betsy, entered the church just fifteen minutes beforehand, accompanied by Reverend Joseph. The few early mourners stepped to the side, so that they could proceed to the place the altar once stood. Betsy stood tall and put her shoulders back; at her age, she had probably seen a lot of death. Her cane swept in front of her and cleared a path. Gretchen looked like hell. Her hair stood out at an odd angle, her eyes were red, and she kept wiping them with a tissue that had been shredded some time ago. They stopped at the front of the church, in front of the display of the urn and the flowers, and stood to face the crowd. Gretchen guided Betsy to a wooden chair, with arms positioned near the urn. Her mother sat in it, propped her hands on her cane, and looked around.

A dozen people showed up at two and formed a line to say a few words and, sometimes, to hug one of the women. After leaving the urn and the picture, they took a seat in the audience and murmured with their neighbors. New Englanders know how to do a funeral.

Things were quiet for the first half hour. I made sure there were enough tissues, asked people to move over to make room for new arrivals, and listened to the docents explain that the names on the stained glass windows were the names of the donors, now long dead too.

About half past two, a thin man, over six feet tall, entered the church and stood just inside the door. He paused and looked around, as if expecting to be recognized. I knew most of Grace's friends and acquaintances, but I didn't recognize him. He looked toward the urn and the flowers and stared for a moment too long at Betsy, sitting in the chair. Betsy seemed to sense his arrival and stared back at him. He started toward the front of the church. As he strode forward, he looked like the stereotypical professor. He was tall and thin, with a halo of white hair. He was even wearing a tweed jacket with patches on the elbows. Much too warm for this weather.

"That's Grace's father," said a voice behind me. "Nathan Connelly."

I turned to see Irene dressed in black from head to toe. "How do you know that?" I whispered.

"He teaches history at the local community college," said Irene, making no effort to whisper. "I took his course there. To hear him talk, you'd think he was tenured at Harvard."

I turned to watch the man, who had now made it to the front of the church. Betsy touched Gretchen's arm, and she turned toward the man. Both nodded and the man, after stopping briefly at the urn, went into the opposite corner from the women.

"That was a bit anticlimactic," said Irene, who had come to stand beside me.

"Did you know he would be here?" I asked.

"I wasn't sure." Irene picked a bit of lint off her black dress. "But I recognized his name, from the obituary, and knew he lived locally. Nathan Connelly, about the right age."

I heard the door open. Armand, the curiosities and collectibles man, arrived with his son, Jesse. They were both dressed like they'd just come from work, in Carhartt pants and boots. Armand took off his hat when he entered the church and he and Jesse made their way to the first easel, with the pictures of Grace as a child. Armand pointed out a few pictures to his son and they moved on to the next easel, with pictures of Grace as a young woman.

"Do you remember her when she was younger?" asked Armand.

He seemed to be talking to his son. Their relationship with Grace had to go back at least a decade if Jesse remembered her; he looked like an adolescent. Maybe they were more than just business acquaintances.

Armand elbowed Jesse in the side. "Come on, you must remember something from back then."

Jesse shrugged and moved away from his father. When he did so, he hit the easel and it clattered against a wooden pew. It was noisy, but both the easel and Jesse righted themselves before there was any damage.

Except for Betsy. She planted her cane between her feet, leaned forward, and got out of her chair. She pushed the cane in front of her to clear the way through the mourners crowded around her. "What are you doing here?" Every head in the church turned. Nobody expected such a loud proclamation from Betsy.

"I'm here to mourn Grace." Armand planted his feet about a foot apart and stared at Betsy.

Jesse took a few steps toward the door. I wanted to join him but my job was to keep things orderly. I noticed that Nathan Connelly had also started toward Betsy's chair.

Betsy pounded her cane on the floor. "Well, don't do it near me," she said. She looked around, realized she was creating a scene, and went back to sit down.

Nathan Connelly stared at Armand. Armand stared back. Both men started back to their respective corners.

"I wonder what that was about," said Irene. "It looks like they know each other."

Armand pulled Jesse into the back pew and they both pretended to read the bulletin that had been printed, setting forth the order of the service and saying a few words about Grace. Not that they seemed to need to know anything more about her.

People went back to their business and the room filled with murmured conversations. More people entered and I was pushed aside. My son was sitting directly on top of my bladder, so I went downstairs for a few minutes before the service started. Returning from my bathroom break, and feeling much better, I started up the stairs. I heard shouting and some scuffling. I hurried upstairs, worried about both the participants and the exhibits. When I got to the top of the stairs, everyone was silent but nothing seemed disturbed. Irene stood between Armand and Jesse.

The pastor was at the front of the room and he clapped his hands. "Now everyone, please take your seats for the service."

Everyone sat down, leaving a wide circle around Armand and his son. My feet were killing me so, for practical reasons rather than to make a statement, I sat next to them. The pastor droned on about Grace, but he didn't seem to have much personal knowledge. He lumped her passion for history in with her dogs and her gardening. He talked about her volunteer work but didn't seem to have much of an idea about the museum or what we did. There was also some praying and some singing. After about forty minutes, the pastor asked if anyone wanted to say some words about Grace.

Everyone looked at each other. No planned speakers; just open conversation. Nobody wanted to go first. After some shuffling of papers and murmuring conversations, Irene stood up. In her black dress she looked like a minister's wife, though not the wife of this minister. She stood behind the podium and spoke in a clear voice. She talked about the Swift River Valley Museum and Grace's love of being here and her passion for all things in her family history. She admitted she didn't know her long, but she gave a much more nuanced picture of Grace than the pastor had. Friends of Grace followed her and talked about Grace as a young girl and as a college student.

After these speeches, the room got quiet. Jesse stood up, stepped over his father, and went into the aisle.

"What are you doing?" The entire congregation heard Armand's question of his son.

"I'm going to talk about Grace." Jesse went to the front of the room and took his place behind the podium. He stared at the assembled mourners.

"I didn't know Grace as long as many of you," he began. "But I knew her well. She worked with my father, she was at the house a lot, and she's done mothering things since my mother died."

Several people turned to their neighbors and made various facial gestures. Armand shifted in his seat.

"It didn't sound like the people who spoke before me knew much about Grace." Jesse looked from the minister to Irene and back. "But she was funny, and she liked to dance to Van Halen and she said 'Oh, Jesse' when she thought I did something stupid. She liked to eat macaroni and cheese and she made cookies from scratch. She said cookies that came in cellophane or from frozen dough were abominations against God."

All the shifting and murmuring had ceased. Jesse had us all mesmerized, not just with his knowledge of Grace, but with his obvious admiration of her.

"I loved Grace," he continued. "She and my dad talked about getting married, and she would be my stepmother."

Betsy gasped. I guess I wasn't the only one that was surprised by that statement. Jesse turned to look at her, still seated in the front of the room.

"It's true," he said. "Grace and my dad were going to get married. Tell them Dad."

Armand was out of his seat and coming to the front of the room. He put his arm around Jesse.

"How could you?" This from Gretchen, who had taken a few steps toward Jesse. "What kind of man are you?"

Armand put a hand on both of Jesse's shoulders and tried to steer him back to his seat.

"No, wait," said Jesse. "I have more to say. I haven't even talked about how we got left out of the obituary completely."

"Not now." Armand tightened his grip on Jesse's arms and led him back to their seats.

Nobody said anything for several seconds, but it seemed like an eternity.

"Thank you all for coming," said the pastor. "Refreshments will be served in the room downstairs." He put out the candles next to Grace's urn and walked to the back of the room. Several mourners got up and started after him.

Armand stopped briefly at the pew where he and Jesse had sat, and apologized as he leaned over me to get his coat. He and Jesse left immediately. I still had work to do, so I went downstairs to the reception.

The church ladies were putting the finishing touches on a spread that included sandwiches, salads, fruit, and cookies. The coffee pot was hot; the cold drinks were on ice. It looked like everything was under control. I grabbed a sandwich and walked out the back door, into the coolness of the late afternoon. Irene followed me out.

"What do you think that was about?" she asked. Not judgmental, just like she was seeking information.

"No idea." I took a bite of the sandwich so I didn't have to say anything else.

"Did you know that Grace and Armand were an item?"

I shook my head, my mouth still full.

"He's a lot older than her, isn't he?" Irene was determined that I would answer her questions. "And what's with Armand and the Connelly guy?"

I swallowed and nodded. "At least twenty years or so. I think Armand was a friend of her mother, Gretchen."

"Do you think that's why Betsy was upset? Because Armand was so much older than Grace? She did seem shocked."

I thought for a moment. I didn't want to start unnecessary gossip. "I don't know" seemed the best answer. Betsy had recovered quickly, but she was obviously upset and angry about what Jesse had said. And, as Grace and Betsy were living in the same house, maybe Grace took steps to keep it a secret. Maybe the truth died with Grace. Or maybe Armand and Jesse knew things about Grace that nobody else did, and more questions needed to be asked.

OBITUARY

Grace Elizabeth Connelly

Grace Elizabeth Connelly, age 42, died on April 22 of this year. She left behind a loving family, loyal friends, and a half a box of Godiva chocolate that she intended to finish. She died suddenly at the Swift River Valley Historical Society, a place she dearly loved.

Grace was the child of Gretchen (Adams) and Nathan Connelly and was named after her grandmother, Elizabeth Grace (Bauman) Adams. She graduated from Mount Herman School for Girls and completed a B.A. degree in English at the University of Massachusetts.

Shortly after obtaining her degree, Grace started her own business "Amazing Grace Curiosities" and she operated a store until 2010, when she moved her business online. She combined her business with her love of history and was on the board of directors of the Swift River Valley Historical Society for over ten years. She told hundreds of school children about the creation of the Quabbin Reservoir and the displacement of people from the towns that were disincorporated. She enjoyed spending time with her family and friends, Godiva chocolate, and her dogs, Dana, Prescott, and Enfield.

A celebration of life will be held on May 3 at the Swift River Valley Historical Society. In lieu of flowers, donations may be made to the historical society.

CHAPTER SIXTEEN

It was almost seven when I got home. Though the sun was not due to set for a few minutes, it was already dark, raw, and overcast; the heat of the day was already gone. It started to rain. And I'd forgotten to turn on the porch light before I left. I pushed open the door and the wind caught it and slammed it shut behind me. Barney looked up when the door slammed, but made no move. Some watchdog.

I yanked the door open again. "Come on, Barney." He still didn't move. "Go outside and do your business. I'll let you right back in."

Barney got up and sniffed at my hand and the bag of Chinese food, getting colder by the minute. He loped to the door and looked back at me. "Go on." He put his front paws on the porch. I pushed the rest of him outside and slammed the door.

I put the food on the counter, got a fork out of the drawer, and dug in. Only lukewarm. Another joy of living in the country: it's twenty minutes to the nearest takeout and it's always cool when it gets home. I plopped the entire contents of the white boxes on a plate and put it into the microwave.

A half-finished wine bottle was still on the counter. I ignored it and sat down at the table to check my phone and see who thought it was important to email me after work hours. I'd barely entered my passcode when the microwave dinged and ninety pounds of dog pushed against the outside of the door.

Standing behind it, to brace myself against the wind, I opened the door about a foot. Barney's massive nose and broad head pushed their way in. I stepped back to let the rest of him enter and spied three people standing on my porch. I flicked on the porch light.

My sister, Hadley, stood on the porch, in a faded dress and a light jacket that didn't keep out any of the night chill. We hadn't talked since the car accident; I kept postponing the call. Her hair was plastered to her head, as if she'd been out in the rain for a while. With her were two smaller people. Meredith, the child I'd pulled from the wrecked car, and an older male child, about ten or eleven. I knew Meredith was my niece and the boy, with his auburn hair, had to be my nephew. In contrast to Hadley, Meredith and her brother were wearing rain ponchos with hoods. Meredith's was a brilliant purple and her brother's was a camo print.

I looked beyond them to a white sedan parked in the yard, with a child's car seat in the back.

"It's a loaner," said Hadley. "They gave it to me while they're fixing the Honda."

As if that would be my first question. What were the three of them doing on my porch? How did they know where to find me? Todd was a police officer and a corrections officer, so his address was not well known. Hell, we weren't even on social media. They all looked miserable.

"Come in," I said. Why would my sister come to do me harm and bring her kids with her? Todd would be home shortly.

Barney greeted them with a tail wave and allowed Meredith to pat him. I shut the door behind them.

"We're dripping all over your floor," said Hadley. "Is there someplace where I can put our wet things?"

"Over there, in the laundry room." I gestured to my right. It took several minutes for everyone to get out of their outside clothes. I brought towels and Hadley dried her hair.

"I was just going to have some dinner," I said. "Have you eaten? I have Chinese takeout."

"I hate Chinese." This from the boy, who crossed his arms over his body.

"Garrett, be nice," Hadley finger combed his hair. "Thank Emma for letting us in and offering us food."

I took the food out of the microwave and divided it between Hadley and me. Hadley made peanut butter and jelly sandwiches for the kids and Barney had to settle for kibble. Hadley refused the wine.

"How did you know where I live?"

Hadley looked around the kitchen. "Grace Connelly told me. Jim and I were looking for a new house and Grace brought me out here. She said the police chief lived here, so it was a safe neighborhood." Hadley removed the mushrooms from her garlic shrimp and set them on the side of her plate. "Of course, we couldn't afford anything in this part of town."

"But how did you know I live here?" Though I hadn't kept track of Hadley, it was apparent that she knew about me.

"The other day," she said. "It was obvious you were a couple, so I took a chance."

I didn't remember making that statement but maybe she just connected the dots. "How are you doing? Any bad effects from the car accident?"

"No, Merry and I are doing fine. Just some cuts and bruises."

"Boo-boo," said Merry. She held up her arm, with two SpongeBob bandages on it.

"I just got home," I said. "How did you know I'd be here?"

"Both Merry and I had cuts from the broken glass." Hadley leaned over and wiped peanut butter off of Meredith's face. "But we're doing better now. Maybe I will have a glass of wine."

I poured the red liquid into the only clean wineglass in the house and put it in front of Hadley. "What are you doing here tonight?"

"She made us come," said Garrett. "I wanted to stay home with Dad, but she said I had to come here." He pushed his half-eaten sandwich away. "And you don't even have good food."

"Garrett, don't say things like that." Hadley stared at her plate.

We needed to have a conversation without the kids. "Do you want to watch television? You can finish your sandwiches while you watch."

We all walked into the living area. The kids sat in front of the screen and Garrett wanted to play *Halo*. I explained that our internet connection wasn't fast enough for gaming. He flipped on the remote to some ghost hunting show that his mother said was too scary for Meredith. They settled on *SpongeBob* and Hadley and I went into the study and closed the door.

"Sit down." I gestured to two chairs placed under the picture window. During the day, it showed a bucolic path to the woods, but now, it reflected the interior, distorted by the lights on the desk. Hadley sat.

"I don't know what I'm doing here." Hadley picked a speck I couldn't see off her dress.

"But I didn't know where else to go and you were so helpful the other day." She looked around the room. "We are family."

We hadn't been a family for several years. And her husband had deliberately sent me away from their part of the family. Several seconds went by.

"Meredith doesn't look like she suffered any harm from her dunking in the stream," I said.

"No, Merry didn't even get a cold. But I wrecked the car and, well, I got these." Hadley pulled up the sleeves of her dress. Her wrists, on both sides, were green and purple with healing bruises.

"How did you get those? When your hand went through the window?"

"No, when I got home." Hadley pulled her sleeves back down over the bruises. "My husband was upset that I took the car and crashed it." She looked around the room and then settled back in the chair. "Things got better when I got the rental car."

None of this made sense. I heard a car pull up in the front of the house.

"Who's that?" Hadley stood up. "Who's coming to the house now?"

"Probably just Todd, the police chief." I thought it was important to include his title, as I was confused about what was going on. "He texted me just before you got here, said he was on his way home." I stood up too. Hadley looked like she could bolt at any second.

"This was a mistake," said Hadley. "I shouldn't have come here tonight." She finished the wine in her glass. "I've got to take the kids and leave."

I didn't hear the garage door open. This fact registered just before I heard a pounding on the front door.

"I've got to go get the kids." Hadley set down the wine glass and left the room.

I looked out the window, but all I saw was my face reflected at me. I stepped out of the study as Garrett rushed by me.

"Mom, it's time to go." Garrett barely finished the sentence when he opened the front door.

The man on the porch was dressed in a canvas jacket and L.L. Bean rubber boots. He was broad shouldered and red faced. Garrett ran to him and put his arms around him. The man bent down and picked up the child. I'd only met Hadley's husband once, at their wedding, but he had to be Jim Mason.

"Daddy, you're here." Garrett laid his head on the man's shoulders. "Now we can go home."

Meredith came out of the living room and stood by her mother, across the table from me. Neither of them said a word, and neither of them took a step toward Garrett and his father.

The man put Garrett on the floor and approached me with an outstretched hand. "I'm Jim. Jim Mason. Don't know if you remember me. I just came to take my family home." He turned to where Hadley and Meredith were standing. "Come here, pumpkin. Come with me."

Meredith left her mother and walked over to her father. Hadley remained where she was.

"Don't you want to come home with us?" Jim directed the question over the heads of the children and directly at Hadley. "The kids need a mother."

I moved over to stand by her. "She and the kids can stay here tonight. If they want to."

Everybody stood still for several seconds.

"I want to go home," said Garrett. "I don't like it here." He pulled open the door.

I moved closer to Jim and was hit with the smell of alcohol and sweat. He pushed past me and took hold of Hadley's wrists. She winced. The cold air from the door blew over all of us.

"I don't want to make a scene. Maybe it's better if we left now." Hadley stepped away from Jim and started gathering up the children's ponchos and her jacket. She looked around for her purse, spotted it on the counter, and went to get it. Hadley was an adult, but I didn't want the kids getting into the car with a man who had been drinking and was visibly upset. And, by the look of Hadley's wrists, had resorted to physical violence.

CHAPTER SEVENTEEN

I stepped between Hadley and Jim. "Why don't they stay here tonight? You've been drinking and they're safer here."

"No, it's okay." Hadley moved past me and the entire family headed out the door and onto the porch.

I followed them out. It was cold and the wind was blowing the rain around. And it was slick underfoot. Hadley took the three steps from the porch to the walkway slowly, followed by Garrett, who jumped down the steps. Meredith came over and took my hand.

Todd's car pulled into the driveway.

At the sight of the cruiser, Jim became more agitated and pulled Garrett and Meredith after him on the path. "C'mon. Let's get out of here." He stumbled on the walk and Garrett fell with him.

Todd got out of the cruiser and hurried over to where Garrett and Jim had fallen and picked up the child by the back of his coat. "What's going on here?"

Jim planted his boots on the walk and stood up. "That's my son and I've come to take him home."

"Have you been drinking, sir?" asked Todd. "It may not be safe for you to drive a car."

"I don't need no cop telling me what to do." Jim tried to push past Todd.

Todd dodged the clumsy push. "That's assaulting a police officer." He stood up to his full height. "Do I have to arrest you?"

I was still on the porch and Hadley joined me there. Meredith came up to stand by her mother.

Garrett pounded on Todd's chest. "Let my father go. He's trying to help."

Todd picked up Garrett, put him over his shoulder, and put him on the porch next to me.

"Leave my son alone." Jim started up the stairs. "This is a family matter."

"It's my family, too," I said. Todd stepped in front of me.

"Listen," said Todd, "I know you're Emma's relations, but I can't let you drive with kids when you've been drinking. Why don't you go home and sleep it off?"

I was standing at the top of the stairs and Jim hip-checked me to get to his family. I lost my footing on the slick boards. Still not used to this pregnant body, I went down with a thud.

Todd ran up the steps, pushing Jim out of the way. He helped me sit up and leaned me against the wall. Jim loomed over us both. Even in the dim light from the single bulb, I could tell he was ready for a fight.

My hip hurt and I couldn't get any leverage to stand up. The slick rain on the porch kept my sneakers from gaining traction. I fell back again, hitting my head on the porch floor. When I reached up, my hair was wet and sticky. Maybe from the rain, maybe from blood.

Todd took a step closer to Jim. Jim pushed him back. Todd went back, right onto my calf. I must have made some noise, because both looked at me.

"I'm fine," I said. "Just don't let him leave with Hadley and the kids."

"They're my kids and my wife." Jim faced Todd. "I'll take them if I want to."

Todd stepped back and rested his hand on his weapon. Jim noticed it too. I was glad only one of them was armed.

"So far, the charge is assault on a police officer and on a pregnant person," said Todd. "If you get behind the wheel of the car, it may be operating under the influence. If you refuse a breathalyzer, it's an automatic suspension of your license to drive."

I looked up at the two men. The nearest breathalyzer was a few towns over, at least a twenty-five-minute drive from here. It would get Jim out of here and busy for a while. Of course, Todd would need to go with him and leave us here alone. Given the possibility of bail and the amount of paperwork Todd would have to do, it was an even bet that Jim would return before Todd. I felt the porch under me, wetting my sweatpants and making me cold down to my bones. I needed to stand up soon.

"Todd, help me up. I'm cold and wet."

Todd came over and helped me stand and led me to a bench still on the porch. It was also cold and wet, but it felt good to sit down.

I whispered to Todd, "Don't leave us alone."

Todd nodded. He often told me that doing what was right and safe did not always mean adhering to the letter of the law.

"You can't order me around." Jim pulled Garrett to his side.

"Well, yes, I can." Todd unhitched the guard on his holster. "But I don't want to. Now, I can drive you home and we can settle it in the morning. Or we can do the field sobriety tests, and I may take you to do a breath test."

"I can't leave my car here. How will I get to work in the morning?"

I thought it interesting that Jim's first concern was for his car, not his family. A little relieved, too.

"You can leave your car here. I'll drive you home and see that it's brought to you in the morning." Todd was using his "reasonable" voice, the one that drove me crazy.

Jim didn't seem to notice. "My family needs to come home with me."

"I'll take you home in my car," said Todd. "I'll get your car to you in the morning. With your family, if they want to come."

Jim lowered his shoulders and stared at the floor. Todd had once described to me the visible signs of someone surrendering, but I'd never seen it so obvious before. Of course, he could be faking it.

"Okay, we'll deal with this in the morning." Jim started down the steps.

Todd came over and knelt by my side. "You okay?" He brushed off my pants and looked me over.

"I can manage," I said. "Just get him out of here."

Todd and Jim got into the car and drove away without incident. I opened the door and Hadley and the kids followed me into the house. I sat down at the table and Hadley checked the back of my head, the only place that appeared to be bleeding.

"It doesn't look too bad, but you should probably clean it," said Hadley, moving my hair from side to side on my head. "And you're shivering. I think you need a shower, to clean up and warm up. If you let me know where you want us, I can put the kids to bed while you shower. Just show me where everything is."

I went to the back closet and brought out sleeping bags and extra pillows for the kids. They could sleep in the guest room. Garrett wanted a tent in the room, but neither Hadley nor I had the ambition to set it up. We spread the sleeping bags on the floor and I went to take a shower.

The shower did make me feel better. The back of my head was tender, but I washed it thoroughly, with only minor discomfort. I checked my pregnant belly and assured my son that I would take care of him.

After my shower, I put on a clean shirt and sweatpants. I rummaged through the bathroom drawers and found hydrogen peroxide, cotton balls, and bandages, in case Hadley wanted to do a little more first aid after she saw my wound.

I walked into the kitchen just as Hadley was finishing the last of the wine. I laid the first aid stuff on the kitchen table. Hadley looked up at me.

"I think I have another bottle of wine, if you want it," I said.

"No thanks," said Hadley. "I've had enough. Do you want some?"

"No, I'm pregnant." I remembered when I said that to Todd, just after meeting Hadley. So much had happened since then. "And I probably shouldn't be drinking with a head injury, anyway."

"How far along are you?" asked Hadley. "We've missed out on so many family milestones."

"I know. I didn't even know that you had two children. Or their names." I sighed, realizing all we had missed.

"Maybe we can start again." Hadley took the glass and wine bottle over to the sink, rinsed them both out, and put them into the dish drainer. "We can be real sisters again."

I sat in the chair and she came over to examine my head. Again, she moved the hair around. This time, it made my scalp tingle.

"Scrubbing the wound has made it red." Hadley pressed the top of my head. "It looks clean to me. I can put hydrogen peroxide on it, but it'll sting. Do you want me to skip that?"

I wasn't making decisions just for me. I couldn't risk infection for the baby. "No, put it on. That's why I brought it out."

She poured the peroxide onto the cotton ball and put it on my scalp. I jumped. She moved back but I signaled her to continue. She applied it again. Better this time.

"That should do it." Hadley threw the cotton balls in the trash and recapped the peroxide. "I don't think you need a bandage; the air is probably better. But you may need a towel on your pillow when you sleep. In case it bleeds again."

Hadley spoke in a low tone, as if to soothe a child. She picked up the unused bandages and put them on the counter. It looked like she might have cleaned the counters and the table when I was in the shower.

"How are you doing?" I asked.

"Okay." She picked up the unused bandages. "Where do you keep these? I'll put them away for you."

"Leave them there. I'll put them away later."

"No trouble, I can do it."

"I think it's more important that we talk. Come sit down." I waved at the chair across from me. "Do you want a cup of tea or coffee or something?"

"No, I'm fine, thank you." Hadley came over to the table and sat down.

Now we were alone, I had no idea how to start this conversation. I didn't want to make any assumptions, or scare Hadley away. I went with my mother's advice: if you don't know what to do, ask. "What can I do to help?"

"Jim and I are going through some hard times, but we'll work it out." Hadley got up, took the dishcloth, and scrubbed a spot on the table. "He's a good father and a good provider. He's just had too much to drink tonight." She went to the sink, hung the dishcloth over the faucet and smoothed it out. "After he sleeps it off, we'll be fine."

"He didn't look fine tonight," I said. "Is this the first time this has happened?"

"Being drunk? No, it's happened before, but only a few times."

I heard a shuffle of feet by the kitchen door. When I turned around, Garrett was standing in the doorway, his arms around his belly.

"Is Daddy coming back to get us tonight?" he asked.

"No, darling." Hadley got up, went over, and put her arms around him. "We're sleeping here tonight."

"I want to sleep in my own bed." Garrett bent over. "My stomach hurts and I don't feel so good."

Hadley brought him to the table, and settled him in her lap. "Do you have anything for a bellyache?"

"Todd has some pink liquid in a bottle. I'll go get it." I went to the bathroom, pulling out random drawers in the cabinet. I opened the medicine cabinet; not there either. Went through the drawers again and found it tucked in the back of the middle drawer.

When I came out of the bathroom, Garrett and Hadley were standing in the hall.

"I don't know about the dosage for kids," I said. "Or even if they should take it."

Hadley took the bottle and read the label. "According to the instructions, Garrett can take a teaspoon. Already got the spoon." She waved one of my own spoons in front of my face. "I'll give it to him now and then we'll go to sleep."

She and Garrett disappeared into their room and shut the door. I gathered our conversation was over. I went into my room and slipped into bed. It seemed large and cold. I turned on the electric blanket, something I usually didn't need with Todd in the bed. It was just getting warm when I heard the bedroom door open and Todd walked in.

"How'd it go?" I asked.

He sat down on the bed and removed his shoes. "Not well. But I think he'll stay at home until morning. I told him if he called a friend to bring him over here, I'll arrest both." He stood up to take off his shirt and pants. "How's Hadley and the kids?"

"Confused," I said. "But I think they're all asleep and safe until tomorrow."

"That's good."

Todd put away his clothes, climbed into bed, put his arms around me. I fell asleep.

I woke to the sound of a car starting.

It was still dark, but Todd snapped on the bedside light. "It's five in the morning. What's going on?" He held his phone in front of my face, as if I needed confirmation of the time.

We both got out of bed, pulled on our sweats, and went to the window. Hadley's car was running in the driveway.

"Did Jim come back to get her?" I asked. "Or is Hadley leaving on her own?" I took the stairs two at a time, ran down the hallway, and pulled open the door. All the bruises from earlier in the evening were hurting.

Hadley's taillights were turning onto the main road.

"It looks like it's just her and the kids in the car." Todd came to stand behind me. "Wherever she's going, we can't stop her now."

"Did she leave a note?" I went into the kitchen and checked the counters and the table, still gleaming from Hadley's efforts last night. I went through the rest of the house, and up to the guest room.

The bed in the guest room was stripped, with the sheets shoved into the pillowcase and sitting on the bed. No trace of Hadley or the children remained; even the wastebasket was empty. The sleeping bags were rolled up and placed at the end of the bed. I went over to them and saw that the sheets and the sleeping bags were covered with pink goo, soaking in and ruining the fabric. An empty bottle of stomach medicine lay on the floor.

CHAPTER EIGHTEEN

Todd entered the room after me. "What a mess. How did this happen?"

"I gave the boy a bottle of stomach medicine last night. Guess he was trying to make a statement." I went over and picked up one of the sleeping bags. "He was upset about not going home with his father." I looked around the room. "Looks like all the bedding needs to be washed. The sleeping bags will need to be professionally cleaned."

"I'll go get garbage bags," said Todd. "Don't want that pink goo on everything." He stopped in the doorway. "Or do you want to go back to bed?"

"I won't be able to sleep now, anyway." I started stuffing the sleeping bags into the bags Todd brought. "That kid, Garrett, was really angry."

I picked up a handful of sheets and started toward the laundry room. Todd picked up towels and other random items and followed me.

"Maybe Hadley went back home because Garrett was so angry," said Todd. "I should probably call later and make sure she's okay."

"Are you sure it was just her and the kids in the car?"

"No." Todd stuffed the towels into the washing machine. "But it looks like she left voluntarily, because she took time to strip the beds and roll up the sleeping bags."

"Yeah, I just wanted to make sure she was safe. Maybe I'll drop in when I'm in town."

"No. Do not go to that house." Todd was using his cop voice. "It's not safe. I'll check on her later."

"I have to go into town anyway," I said. "You're right, but she's my sister, even if we haven't seen each other for years. I'll call, not go over."

"Can I trust you to stay away from Jim Mason and his family?"

I sighed. "Of course I'm going to stay away. I know how dangerous abusive men can be. And now I have to protect my child too."

Todd came over and put his arms around me. "I know this is tough for you. Having Hadley here can bring up bad memories. But I will protect you and our baby. I just need some time to get used to the idea of a family."

He pulled away from me and I noticed pink goo on his shirtsleeve. "You have stuff on your shirt." Todd looked down and started unbuttoning his cuffs. "Another reason not to have kids," he said. His hands stopped when he realized what he said.

"I'm sorry, Emma. For a guy who's good at getting other people to talk, I'm making a mess of this. It's just, I've done parenting before, and it's hard and I'm old. Sometimes how hard it is just overwhelms me."

"I know," I said. "Just, it's important to me to know where we're going."

"I want you to know I'll be with you, no matter what. Let's get engaged, then we can show the world that we're a couple. I'll buy you a diamond this weekend."

"Don't want a diamond." I took the shirt from him, put it in the washer, added detergent, and started the machine. "I hate diamonds.

Couldn't wait to get rid of the huge rock that my first husband gave me. Like a payment for services rendered."

"Good to know," said Todd. "See how well it works when you tell me what you want. Oh yeah, you didn't tell me what you want. Just what you don't want."

I smiled. I couldn't help myself. "I'd like a stone with some color. A sapphire or an emerald. No cold, white stones."

"I'll make a note of it. Let me know what you want, what the baby needs. I'll get it."

And that was the problem. I didn't want to have to ask. I wanted him to offer. I wasn't even sure what I wanted him to offer. It was so confusing.

"I'm going to get a clean shirt and get to work," said Todd. "I'll check on Hadley later today and let you know what I find out."

"I've got to get going too."

"Are you still planning to go into town?" Todd looked like he was ready to fight about it.

"Yeah," I said. "But I'll stay away from Hadley. I think it's about time I had a talk with Kevin Angetti."

"Kevin Angetti? The kid at the museum?"

"Trooper Gray keeps calling him a suspect. I want to see what his story is."

Todd had on his cop face again.

"Don't worry," I said. "I'm going to the garage, have my tires checked. I won't be alone with him."

CHAPTER NINETEEN

Kevin was in the yard when I pulled into the garage. My left front tire had been looking a little flat. Of course, living in the country, I knew how to use a tire gauge and could have checked it myself but, if it was flat, I still needed to add air to it or get it patched.

I walked over to where Kevin had a tire on a round wheel, to separate it from the rim. He didn't look up when I approached. Social skills were not a strong point, unless he was talking about the history that he loved.

"Hey, Kevin," I said. "How are you doing?" Not exactly an original greeting, but it worked for him.

He looked up and nodded his head. "Hi, Emma. What are you doing here today?" In Kevin's world, that was an enthusiastic welcome.

"Tires are a little flat. I was hoping you could check the numbers and add some air, if it's needed."

"Not a problem," said Kevin. "Just let me finish doing this. It'll take a few minutes." He went back to wrestling the tire from its rim.

"The cops have been to the museum a few times to talk to me," I said. "About Grace and the missing items."

"Talked to me too." Kevin didn't look in my direction, concentrating on his task. "I didn't like it."

"It wasn't much fun for me, either. They had some documents they found under Grace and in the barn. Wanted to know how they got there."

Kevin's head came up and he looked directly at me. "How would I know about that?" He seemed to realize he'd made eye contact and dropped his head. "I mean, were the documents damaged? We need to do our best to preserve everything as it is."

"Yes, we do. I'd like to talk to you about that. Will you be taking a break soon? I'll buy you coffee at the diner."

Kevin took the tire off the round device and dropped it on the ground. "My family owns this place; I can take a break when I want. Let me put this away, check your tires, and we can go for a short break." This was more words than I had heard Kevin say, unscripted, since I met him. He rolled the tire into the garage, shouted at some relative, checked my tires, and told me they were fine.

Within ten minutes, we were sitting in the diner with coffee in front of us. The coffee here was uneven, to be charitable, but I didn't want Kevin, or one of his relatives, to decide that a longer break was a problem.

"Do you want something to eat? Toast or an English muffin?" Todd told me, years ago, that the way to get people to talk to you was to feed them. The younger the person, the more likely it was to work.

"No thanks." Kevin added four teaspoons of sugar to his coffee. "I'm fine. What did you want to talk to me about?"

"There's so much going on at the museum, I'm trying to talk to everyone about what's going on. Irene and I spoke the other day. Of course, most of that conversation was about history. Always seems to be about the history."

Kevin nodded but didn't say anything.

"Let's start at the beginning. Is there any way you could have made a mistake about what was missing? When you did the April inventory?"

"Nobody's perfect." Kevin stared out the window. The only things moving outside were the cars on the street and a stray dog inspecting the sidewalk. The parking lot was in the back, out of sight, but nobody appeared to go back there. "But I'm really careful about counting and recording. The ice equipment and the documents could be somewhere else at the museum, but they weren't where they were supposed to be. That's what I noted in the inventory."

"Do you think Grace took the items? Is that something she would do?"

No hesitation. "No way," he said. "She wanted things to stay in the museum and to be shared with the public." He stared out the window again.

"But," I said.

He hesitated this time. "But," he said, "she and Armand, you know the Armand's Collectibles guy, they had something going to jack up the prices of stuff not in the museum. They needed money and they talked about ways to get more things at cheaper prices." Another long speech from Kevin. This was a day of surprises.

"How do you know that?" I asked. "Were you at the museum when Armand and Grace were there?"

"No." Kevin stared out the window again. He really was a bad liar. "But I heard it from somebody else."

"Who? And how did they know?"

"I can't say," said Kevin. "I promised." I hoped he would say more, but now he was staring into his coffee cup. I thought it interesting that he would lie about what he knew, but keep confidences of other people.

"The police keep telling me that you are a suspect." I decided to be as blunt as possible. "Because of the trouble your family gets into."

Kevin moved his lips and I thought he was going to tell me what was going on. "I'm not my family," he said. But he didn't deny his family had been in trouble.

Kevin was socially awkward and I didn't know how much of his hesitations and mannerisms were because of his inability to read other people or how much he was trying to cover up. "Kevin, you and I have known each other for years. What is going on?"

"My dad said I shouldn't talk about it."

Kevin lived with his aunt and uncle and, in all the years I'd watched him grow up, I'd only seen his father a handful of times. "What was your father doing in town?"

"He came to see me. And he and Uncle Al had some kind of business deal going on. They went to the bank."

Kevin's father had been selling drugs out of his mechanic shop; he also chopped up stolen cars. Kevin resided with his aunt and uncle while his dad was in jail and just stayed on after his release. Maybe their business was legitimate, but I wasn't sure. I just hoped it didn't include Kevin.

"Well, I've got to go," said Kevin. "Break time is over." He took out some one-dollar bills and put them on the table.

"Kevin, I'll pay for your coffee."

"My family pays its own way," he said. He recited it like it was the family motto. "We don't take charity."

"Are you doing okay?" That sounded lame, even as I said it. "I mean, you're not in any trouble, are you? You had nothing to do with the missing items?"

"I had nothing to do with the missing items." He didn't deny that he was in trouble, though. And he was lying about something. I followed him out of the diner.

In the parking lot, someone had poured black grease all over my car. And there was a note under the windshield.

CHAPTER TWENTY

I called Todd and the police. Todd arrived first. He went into the cruiser, brought out latex gloves, and took the note off the windshield. He then walked around the car. "What a mess," he said.

My first instinct was to tear the note off the windshield. Todd's solution was much more procedurally correct. "What does the note say?" I asked.

"Stop sticking your nose into other people's business and asking questions. Somebody could get hurt or die." Todd held the paper out to me, took a paper bag out of the car, and dropped the note into it. He took several pictures of the car with his phone.

"Can I look at the note again?" I asked.

Todd stopped pacing and looked at me. "Why? What do you think you'll see?"

"Just humor me," I said. He handed me a pair of gloves and I put them on and took the note out of the bag. It was Times New Roman typeface, a little larger than standard. And, of course, not signed. "It's the ampersand," I said.

"The what?" Todd asked. "Does it have an identifying mark?"

"No," I said. "It's a symbol, above the seven on a standard keyboard. And it's unusual. Most people would've just typed out 'and,' not put in an ampersand."

"Is this important?" Todd's phone rang and he declined the call.

"It is, because I recently met a person who went into detail about an ampersand. How it was created by monks who copied books in Latin. It is a combination of the letters 'e' and 't', which means 'and' in Latin." My conversation with Jesse came back to me. "Like you, many people don't know what an ampersand is. But Armand LaValley and his son, Jesse, are fascinated and included one in their name."

Todd put the note back in the bag. "I think I'll have to have a talk with Mr. LaValley."

And then the police cruiser arrived. One patrol officer, who implied that he had better things to do. Guess a small-town police chief didn't impress him; he left after less than fifteen minutes. We used the winter ice scraper, kept in the car year-round in New England, to get the black gunk off the windshield. We drove to the car wash and gave it a good cleaning.

CHAPTER TWENTY-ONE

I was dreaming about babies. Plump, pink babies, floating in the air, just waiting for me to pick out the one that would be born to me. Little girls with pink bows, little boys in overalls, and genderless children with bow lips and tiny fingernails. A buzzer sounded. Was it time for me to pick? It sounded again.

"Are you going to answer that?" Todd rolled over and grumbled in my ear.

No more fat babies. My phone was ringing. Not ringing, buzzing. That meant the call was from someone not on my caller list. I brought it up to my face. Seven twenty-one on a Saturday morning. I was already awake, so I decided to answer it. In the back of my mind, I knew no good news came from a stranger early in the morning.

"Emma? Emma Wetherby?" said a voice I almost recognized.

"This is Emma. Who am I talking to?"

"Did I wake you up? Oh, I'm so sorry, but he's going to be here at eight this morning."

I got out of bed, walked into the hallway, and closed the door. No need for Todd to be up also. "Who is this?" I asked.

"I wanted to call you before he got here. Armand LaValley, I mean. He's coming here this morning." I heard scuffling and pages turning. "It's Betsy. Betsy Adams, Grace's grandmother."

That cleared up who I was talking to, but I still had no idea why she called. "Mrs. Adams, what about Armand LaValley? Do you know him and why is he coming today?"

"Of course I know him. He's the antique dealer that Grace works with. Armand's Curiosities and Collectibles. He said he met you. And he's coming here and I think you should be here too."

I thought back to my previous interaction with Armand and had my doubts about whether I wanted to meet him again. I knew Betsy Adams was no match for him. "Why is he coming over to your house so early on a Saturday?" I hoped she answered my question this time.

Todd opened the bedroom door. "What are you doing out in the hallway?" So much for not disturbing his sleep.

I put my hand over the phone. "Talking to Betsy Adams. I'm not sure what she wants."

"Come into the kitchen and put your phone on speaker." Todd took my arm and we went downstairs. He sat me at the table and I pressed the button on the phone.

Mrs. Adams was in the middle of a sentence when I got back to her. "—and he said that he hadn't paid for the items, and he didn't want any trouble with the police."

"Mrs. Adams, please go over that again. I don't understand why Armand is coming to your house and what it has to do with me."

"Call me Betsy, please. Gretchen was going through Grace's records. She's so much better at that than I am. She said she didn't want to bother me, because I'm old. Okay, she didn't say old, but that's what she meant. But I wasn't any good at numbers, even when I was younger. Organizing events and kids and appointments, that's what I'm good at."

Todd sat down across from me and raised his eyebrows. I waved my hands and mouthed "I can't figure it out either." Betsy just kept talking.

"When Gretchen, that's my daughter, you know, Grace's mother." I did know, but Betsy said it anyway. "When she was going through the records, Grace seemed to be selling a lot more stuff than she was buying. Not just money, it would be normal that she sold stuff for more than she bought it. But she had a larger number of items sold than bought. Mostly to Armand. Now, I'm not saying that Grace was stealing stuff, but maybe Armand was manipulating her."

Maybe Grace was stealing stuff, I thought. Todd got up from the table, got mugs out of the cupboard, and poured a cup of coffee for both of us.

"So, Gretchen called to ask him. Last night, late. He said he would be over at eight this morning to discuss it," said Betsy. "I don't like it and thought maybe you and the police chief could come over. I don't have his number and it's not an emergency, so I didn't want to call 911. When I called the police dispatcher, she wasn't very nice to me. But I knew your number and that's when I made a call."

At last, the reason for the call. I looked at Todd and he nodded.

"We'll be there in about a half hour," I said.

"Please hurry. I want you here before he arrives." Betsy hung up.

Todd and I pulled into the Connelly yard. No sign of Armand. The front door banged open and Gretchen came out into the yard, dressed in just her jeans and a lightweight jacket. No shoes and it didn't look like she wore much under the jacket.

"My mother called you, didn't she?" Gretchen started talking before she got to us. "I told her not to bother you."

"No bother," said Todd. "If the accounts don't match, we'd want to talk to him anyway." No mention of our mad scramble to get dressed and here before Armand.

"The thing is, I'm not sure if there is a discrepancy." Gretchen pulled the jacket tighter around her shoulders. "Grace could have had things given to her or she could have paid cash for some stuff."

Before we had a chance to inquire further, Armand's truck pulled into the yard. He was alone today; no sign of his son. He swung out of the cab and came over to where we were standing.

"Didn't know the chief was going to be here." He put his hand out and Todd shook it. "But I guess that means we can clear up everything today."

"That would be good," said Todd. He turned to Gretchen. "Can we go into the house, where it's warmer?"

"No problem. I made coffee." Gretchen led us onto the porch and inside the house.

Betsy was sitting at the kitchen table, the dogs at her feet. When we entered, the dogs got up and sniffed each of us in turn, then went back to sit with Betsy. She was fully dressed, down to the laced Red Wing boots on her feet. We joined her. Todd and I declined more coffee, but Gretchen zipped up her jacket and made a cup for Armand. Seems my life, recently, was measured in coffee cups.

"So, why are we here?" Todd looked around the table.

Betsy looked down. Gretchen turned to Armand, who stared back.

"When I was looking over Grace's records, I found some problems." Gretchen continued to look at Armand, who then folded his hands around his coffee cup.

"What kind of problems?" asked Todd.

"Grace seemed to be selling a lot more items than she bought. Her online sales seemed balanced, but she sold a lot of stuff to Armand and didn't have a record of where she got it."

"I'm an honest businessman." Armand slapped his hand on the table. "I have receipts for everything I bought from Grace. And I have records of who I sold it to."

"All of it?" asked Todd. "Even cash sales?"

Armand stared out the window. "I have a computer program. Some sales are just cash, with no name. But they're all in the system."

"Did you ask Grace where she got the items she sold you?" I asked. Todd looked over at me, but I'm an archivist, this is what I do. And I wanted the question answered.

"Sometimes. But I get lots of stuff when people clean out their parents' or grandparents' houses. Buy the stuff in bulk, don't ask where it came from." Armand took a sip of coffee. "Assumed Grace did the same thing."

"Exactly what was the relationship between you and Grace?" Todd asked. "Jesse said that you were going to get married."

"Damn kid, don't know what he's talking about," said Armand. "That's why I didn't bring him with me today. He causes more trouble than he's worth."

Now I was confused. Jesse seemed so sure. "You mean you weren't going to get married? Where did he get the idea that you were?"

"Jesse is sometimes slow to catch on to what's happening," said Armand. "Grace and I never did anything illegal, but sometimes we played up our relationship, you know, to get prices down."

"How did that work?" asked Todd.

Armand looked at the ground. "You know, like acting," he said.

"No," said Todd. "I don't know. What did you do or say?"

"Well, sometimes we'd act like a married couple," said Armand. "Like we were looking for things that belonged to Grace's grandparents that had been given away by mistake. Then she'd see something else, make like it reminded her of her grandma. With older people, whose kids probably didn't want it anyway, they sometimes offered to give it away."

Todd crossed his arms. Armand continued talking. "And sometimes we'd be father and daughter, looking for the same things. Depended on what we thought would work with the person selling."

"Were you and Grace involved?" I asked.

"No. Not in that way," said Armand. "I treated her like a daughter. A daughter I wanted to take care of."

Armand looked at Gretchen, who leaned down to pat the dogs. Something was going on between them; they seemed to be communicating with just looks.

"You might as well tell them," said Gretchen. "With what Grace uncovered, too many people know anyway."

Betsy snorted.

Armand got up and went to stand by Gretchen. "Before Grace was born, Gretchen and I were a couple for a few years after high school. I thought of Grace as more of a daughter. She liked to spend time with me, and Jesse, and he got the wrong idea."

Todd took out his notebook. "Is Grace your daughter?"

"No." Gretchen's denial was immediate and loud. "Grace was born ten years after Armand and I broke up. She's Nathan's child. She even looks, looked, like him."

"So what did Grace find that brought this all up?" Todd asked.

"Papers, always old papers." Armand shook his head. "Gretchen almost made the Olympic team, back in the sixties and seventies. She kept articles on her and the team. One picture, in *Life*, I think, showed the two of us together. Grace asked and I told her that Gretchen and I separated so that she could concentrate on her swimming."

"Why don't you say it?" asked Betsy. "I made sure you weren't together, so Gretchen could follow her dream."

Armand put his hand on Gretchen's shoulder. "It did seem you were hellbent on her not being with me. You even got her a coach forty miles away so she wouldn't be around town."

"I got her a coach so she could be the best at what she did." Betsy slammed the table. "She needed to practice, not hang out with you or any other boy."

I directed my question at Armand. "Did you and Gretchen ever get back together?"

"No." He went around the table and retook his seat. "When she didn't make the Olympics, I'd already married Martha, my first wife. I've had three of them."

Probably his wives were younger than him. He was over sixty and Jesse was just a teenager. Maybe he was hoping to capture something he thought he missed out on. I tried to figure out how it fit into the story of Grace's murder, but didn't come up with any ideas. Meanwhile, Todd had moved on in his questioning.

"Do you mind if we go through your records?" asked Todd.

"Of course I mind." Armand stood up. "I came here to be helpful, not to be accused. You got any more questions, talk to my lawyer."

"Who is your lawyer?" asked Todd.

"I'll let you know as soon as I get one." Armand turned and left the room. We all heard his footsteps as he crossed the porch. His truck started and he was gone.

CHAPTER TWENTY-TWO

I spent the rest of the day at the museum, filing documents, preparing for our donor campaign, and posting our summer schedule to social media and local newspapers and radio. I checked the lock on the barn, again, and called Irene to make sure the alarm people had come to update the system. I didn't like feeling scared in the place that had been my refuge. But things needed to be done.

None of the work took great concentration, and my thoughts kept returning to Armand and his denials about, well, everything. He knew Grace best and, through my years of watching cop shows, I knew to look at the family first. Even if he was not Grace's boyfriend, he was in a good position to kill her.

Boyfriend. That seemed an outdated term for an adult relationship. But what was the alternative? Significant other, paramour, lover? None of them quite fit. Todd and I had struggled with defining our relationship for years.

Todd was a guardian. When I accepted that fact about him, I grew to love him. He is often direct, and abrupt, and suspicious of everyone. He is also suspicious about human relationships, even the ones that are not romantic, because he has seen so many of them go wrong. But he is protective of everyone and will go out of his way to make sure everybody gets a fair deal. To quote his favorite fictional character, Harry Bosch, everybody matters or nobody matters.

My thoughts were going around and around in my head. I wasn't even concentrating on Grace's murder, I was examining my relationship and analyzing Todd and his motives. I decided to go home early and start again tomorrow.

When I got home, I was greeted with the aroma of tomatoes and basil. Todd stood in the kitchen, wearing my apron, the one with the runaway forks and spoons on it.

I opened the closet to put away my coat and purse. "Nice apron."

Todd looked down at himself, as if noticing it for the first time. "This old thing? I needed something to stop the pasta sauce from splashing on me. First thing I found."

I sat down at the counter and he put a glass of sparkling water in front of me. "What are you doing making dinner?"

"It's my day off from the house of correction, and I finished my police chief work early." It was an indication of how frazzled I was that I forgot his day off.

"What can I do to help?" I asked.

"Nothing," he said. "It just needs to simmer in the pot for a while. I like that instant pot; I don't even have to watch it." He'd mangled the name, but I got the idea. "I thought I'd just leave it to do its thing while I walk Barney."

As if summoned by his name, Barney sauntered into the room and stretched. I got the leash and attached it to his collar. There were too many temptations for him when we walked the country roads. "I think I'll go with you."

Todd nodded and we left. Walking in New England is one of the best experiences of my life. I do enjoy fall, with the spectacular foliage display, but May, with all the trees and bushes in bloom, is hard to beat. We walked slowly, as Barney needed to stop at every stump, bush, and clump of grass to see what animals had been there before. The squirrels and chipmunks were out in force, so I was glad Barney was on his leash.

"Can't beat this," said Todd. "Walking in the woods, with my woman and my dog."

That statement was so unlike Todd that I couldn't decide which part of it to respond to first. Should I be insulted or flattered that he called me his woman? Or should I praise him for sharing his emotions, something he did so seldom? Or should I just agree that this was a great time outdoors. Before I could make up my mind, he started talking again.

"I'm confused. And angry." Todd followed Barney behind a tree and I lost the next few words. He came back out and went right on talking. "I want things to be easy. I want to live with you, and have a perfect child, and have Dierdre and Brian be happy. And I don't want to be upset at what's going on." He pulled Barney onto the trail and put his arm around my waist. It felt good being near him, but Barney had other ideas. It was his walk, after all.

"Say something," said Todd. Barney pulled at the leash.

"I want the same things you do, for everybody to be happy and satisfied," I said. "But it's not easy. Maybe it's my history with my first husband, but putting things off until they get better never works. Something else will come up. You need to do what you need to do, right now."

"I know that, but sometimes it's hard to remember when life overwhelms you." Todd looked so forlorn after that statement that I reached up and kissed him. He put his arms around me and deepened the kiss. And I remembered why I wanted to be with this man.

"Let's go home," he said. Even Barney cooperated, seeming to be less interested in his surroundings now we were headed home.

Todd went over to check on the sauce. "I'm hungry," he said. "For food and for you."

I laughed. "Well, at least you're honest about it."

He put the lid back on the sauce. "Will this stuff keep in the pot?"

"Yeah," I said. "It'll keep for hours." That was a good thing, because we didn't get around to the pasta until almost midnight.

CHAPTER TWENTY-THREE

I woke alone the next morning. I'd slept until ten, something I almost never do. And I awoke to the smell of eggs and bacon. My morning sickness seemed to have resolved, because I was hungry, even after the midnight pasta snack. I skipped the shower, because I hate cold eggs and bacon. Todd was in the kitchen, again wearing my apron; the only other item of clothing he had on was his running shorts. There was still a chill in the early morning, but he didn't seem to care. And I appreciated the sight.

He turned to look at me. "Bacon and eggs are ready."

"Yeah, I smelled them." I sat down at the table. "Skipped my shower, so they wouldn't get cold. Anyway, it's always better to shower after bacon." Todd placed two plates and two cups of coffee on the table. "Why this sudden burst of domesticity?" I asked.

"Well, last night it got me something great. And I'm smart enough to repeat behavior that has a positive outcome." He sat down in his chair. "And, in all the excitement of last night, I forgot to tell you about my meeting with Nathan Connelly."

"Nathan Connelly?" I couldn't place the name. "Some relation to Grace?"

"Grace's father," Todd said. "He was at the funeral."

"Tall man, looked like a professor? I think Irene pointed him out to me."

"He called the police number, asked to see me. Said he had news about Grace." Todd took a bite of his toast and chewed it slowly.

"And?" I made the rolling wrist gesture to move him along.

"Oh, you want to know what he said?" Todd grinned. "What are you willing to give me for the information?"

"You give me the information and, if it's any good, I'll reward you later."

"I'll think about how I want to be rewarded." Todd nodded. "He said that Grace had called him the day before she died and they met. This was unusual, because they go months without talking and then it's generally just an exchange of plans. Nathan said that he couldn't ever remember Grace calling him, and asking to meet, before."

"I remember the divorce, though I was several grades behind Grace. It upset her and she blamed it all on her father," I said. "It's not surprising they don't talk much."

"Do you want to hear my story or should I finish my breakfast?" He took another bite and did that chewing forever thing.

"Just wanted to give you some history," I said. "Because you're so much older than I am."

"I kept up with you last night," he said. "You're blushing, just thinking about it." He was right, I was blushing, but he didn't need to point it out. "Grace wanted to talk to him about the results of a DNA test she took. Said it showed she had a half-sibling, and she wanted to talk to him about the women he'd been with, during and after his marriage to her mother. Nathan swore he knew nothing about another child, but Grace was adamant."

"And then?"

"And then, nothing. Nobody can find the DNA test she was talking about. Maybe she made the whole thing up."

"Or maybe Nathan is lying." Men lie; I knew that from my past marriage.

"Maybe," said Todd. "But I've got to track it down anyway. That means notifying all the places that do paternity testing and asking them for the results. Or getting subpoenas for the results."

"So you are back on the case?" This surprised me, that he had knowledge about this ongoing investigation, given his conflict of interest.

"No," he said. "But they are letting me do the tracking work. When it comes to actually contacting the labs, they will have someone else do it. I'm relegated to research only." He sounded bitter, but resigned.

"Was Nathan any help? Did he see the tests; does he know where they were done?"

"He says he doesn't know, or he's not sharing with us. So I need to start the tedious task of making a list of all the paternity labs. I'll start with Google, and hope Grace started there too. But first, Carol is coming over to talk to me."

"Carol? About the wedding?" Todd was so upset about Brian and Dierdre getting married, I couldn't image that he'd want to talk to his ex-wife about it.

"Yeah, I guess part of being a father is dealing with the hard stuff."

CHAPTER TWENTY-FOUR

Carol arrived shortly after we got home. I often wondered if Carol and Todd bonded over their obsessions with being on time and their straightforward approach to problem-solving. I'm always running late, but I do keep to-do lists and schedules, so at least I make an attempt. Carol wore a navy-blue pantsuit, with a striped shirt and low heels. Very much the successful woman on the go. I'd heard horror stories about their marriage from Todd, but tonight I needed to support her in her efforts to get this wedding on track and to deal with Todd's feelings about Brian and Dierdre getting married.

We all sat at the table and Carol declined an offer of wine. She asked for water and I joined her in that drink. Todd sat at the table and drummed his fingers on the surface. He must have been nervous; he seldom had any obvious tells.

"I've come to talk about Brian and Dierdre's wedding," said Carol. That seemed obvious, or perhaps she was just laying the ground rules and starting with something we could all agree on. We did need to talk about the wedding. "Brian and Dierdre are adults and can legally marry. Whatever our personal feelings, we need to support them on this day."

Todd stopped the drumming. "But they were raised as brother and sister. Them getting married, it seems, I don't know, unnatural."

"Unnatural?" Carol was very good at expressing skepticism. Or was it ridicule? She seemed to display a little of both. "They may be ahead of many new couples. They know what it's like to live together, they've had years to adapt to being together, and, as a bonus, they don't have to take on an unknown set of in-laws."

I smiled at the last remark. Todd did not.

"If we stand together, maybe we can talk them out of this," he said. "Or at least slow it down, so they have more time to think it through. Everything is just moving too fast."

"You do know that Dierdre is pregnant, right?" Carol stared at Todd, as if this fact might have escaped him. When he nodded, she continued. "Maybe I'm a bit out of fashion about this, but I think a child should have parents that are married, and committed to each other, as well as the child."

Now I stared at Todd. He winced.

"What's the matter?" asked Carol. "Don't you think the child is Brian's? Dierdre said that you asked. I know my children; they are devoted to each other."

"No," said Todd. "That's not it at all."

To hell with secrets. Besides, Todd told me not to tell Dierdre and Brian. He'd said nothing about Carol. A minor point, I guess, but they were going to figure it out soon. "I'm pregnant," I said. "I'm due the month before Dierdre."

Todd started drumming his fingers on the table again. Carol was the first to speak. "You're pregnant? How long have you known? Brian never mentioned it."

"Brian doesn't know," I said. "Neither does Dierdre. We were waiting to tell them."

"Waiting for what?" asked Carol. She stopped talking for several seconds. "I guess their wedding was a shock and you didn't need to tell them about another complication."

Damn, why did she have to be so understanding of Todd's position? She sounded like him; I can see why they got along. I didn't like the idea that she'd already got to parent with Todd, but she was making this awkward situation easier.

"So, when are you getting married? Have you chosen a date?" Carol looked from Todd to me. "We shouldn't have both weddings in the same month."

"We're not sure we're getting married," said Todd.

"Why not?" Carol raised her voice. "Didn't you hear the part about a child needing two parents who are committed to each other?" Neither Todd nor I said anything. "You are committed to each other, aren't you?"

This family stuff was hard. I'd always thought I had it tough, with a dead mother, a distant father, a brother in and out of jail, and a sister I'd lost touch with for years. Sometimes it was harder to have a family around, getting into your business and asking difficult questions. Not that I hadn't asked all these questions myself.

Todd stood up. "Do you want more water?" he asked the room in general.

"No, I don't need any more water," said Carol. "I need you to answer my question. Are you committed to Emma and this baby?"

"I'm committed to all my kids," said Todd. "I want this baby to be healthy, and I want Brian and Dierdre to be happy. Sometimes it's just difficult to know what the right thing is to do."

"I can't help you and Emma resolve your problems." Carol pulled papers from her purse and put them on the table. "But I can plan a decent wedding for Brian and Dierdre. And you're going to help me."

It was a relief to stop talking about my pregnancy and talk about definite plans for a definite event. Carol was a force of nature and she had talked to Dierdre about her plans and wishes. By the end of the evening, we had a tentative date and a list of venues for Carol and Dierdre to visit. Todd had agreed to be part of the ceremony and keep his doubts about the wedding to himself. If he could support his children in something he disagreed with, I saw that as a good sign for us.

June

CHAPTER TWENTY-FIVE

June came in like summer. We went from mud season and overcast skies to sunshine and birds. The grass didn't quite make the transition; it was still brown and patchy. But I didn't want to get out of bed. Todd put his arm around me and I snuggled further down in the bed. Then, I felt it. A slight movement, almost like someone had run their hand over my skin. Todd's hand was on my belly, but it wasn't moving.

"What was that?" he asked.

"The baby. He moved." As I said it, I felt the sensation again.

"Isn't it a little early for the baby to be moving?" Todd sat up and looked over at me.

"Our child is a quick learner. He's growing on his own timetable."

Todd got out of bed. "We can tell Dr. Nancy at the appointment today. She's going to encourage us to attend the Down syndrome support group. What do you think?"

The thought of another item on my already full to-do list was not appealing. "I really don't want to sit around and hear other people's stories," I said. "Let's just concentrate on making our own."

"And maybe we're worrying for nothing," said Todd. "The tests aren't conclusive, maybe there won't be a problem."

Cop reaction, that's what Todd's face revealed. I recognized it immediately. When out on patrol, a cop doesn't know what will happen next, or which situations will be dangerous. So he remains alert and on guard, looking for trouble but not preparing for a specific threat. I don't know about other cops, but Todd showed this behavior on a regular basis. And I gave my standard answer.

"We'll see. Right now, I need to get out of bed and meet the troopers."

"And I have to get to work." Todd got dressed and left the room.

Contrary to what I said, I stayed in bed until I heard the door slam and Todd start his truck. I got dressed and made sure the note I had received was secure in its plastic sleeve. It was a copy—the town cops had the original—but I wanted to keep it as I got it. We were meeting, once again, at the historical society. I don't know whether the troopers were checking up on the scene of the crime, or if they did it for my convenience, but I was glad I didn't have to drive to the nearest barracks.

I was back at the historical society to meet with the troopers. Bachelor and Gray once again. I'd told them about the threatening note and Armand's visits. They said they'd followed up and now had some more questions for me. The cruiser was parked in the lot when I pulled in. The troopers were talking near the back steps. Trooper Gray was waving her hands. Both stopped talking and turned when I got out of my car.

"Good morning," said Trooper Gray. "Could we look at the murder scene and the barn before we talk?"

I stopped walking and shook my head. I'd never actually heard anyone refer to the museum as a murder scene. Of course, they might have used the term on the confusing day of the event and I didn't remember. "Why do you want to do that?"

"We need to look in the house again." This wasn't really an explanation, just Gray restating what she already said.

"Of course." I went through my purse, looking for my keys. "But the room has been cleaned and the rug removed. We're open now, so we scrubbed the area."

"Not a problem," said Gray, as she exchanged a look with Bachelor. "I'd just like you to point out what was missing from the room."

"There was nothing missing from the room where Grace was found." There had been police reports and insurance reports, didn't Gray read them? Maybe I was being unfair; she had other cases besides Grace's murder. "We've completed the inventory and the missing items were from the map room and upstairs in the house."

"The map room?" This question came from Bachelor.

"Used to be the breakfast room," I said. "We call it the map room because of a papier-mâché model of the valley before it was flooded. It also has paper maps, pictures, and books. Some paintings were also missing from the upstairs."

"Did you file a police report on the missing items?"

"Weeks ago," I said. "We had to file with the police before the insurance company would process the claim."

"How much was the insurance claim?" asked Bachelor.

"Only a few thousand dollars." Not worth killing someone for.

We'd now reached the Enfield Room and Gray started walking around it, clockwise from the hallway door. "Nothing was missing from here?"

"No," I said. "And we did a complete inventory."

Gray stopped pacing. "Okay, let's go see the barn."

"Why the barn?" There was nothing in there but broken furniture and used pallets.

Bachelor and Gray looked at each other. I didn't like the feeling that I'd been excluded from important information. I was in charge of the museum and I had a right to know what was going on. I don't know whether they sensed my anger, but Gray decided to share information.

"We found a print on the peanut butter jar in the barn," she said. "An individual named Steven Milford. Do you know him?"

I took a moment to run through the people I'd met in the last few months. Because the museum had been closed, it was a short list. "No, I don't think I know the name."

Bachelor pulled out a picture and showed it to me. "If you don't recall the name, do you know the face?"

I'm better at faces, but it didn't look familiar. Then another thought came to me. "You've had the items from the barn for over a month. Didn't you know this information before now?"

"Of course," said Gray. "But we had to check some things out before we shared them with the public."

So much for my being in the loop. We made it to the barn and I unlocked the door. The sleeping bag and food were gone but, other than these changes, the barn looked the same as it always had. Old, broken furniture piled in the back, along with blankets and broken tools. Gray and Bachelor started by the door and walked in ever-widening circles, much as they had done in the Enfield Room. They walked slowly and didn't stop, except to move a few pieces of furniture.

"Do you see anything out of place?" asked Bachelor. "Anything added or missing. What did the inventory show?"

"We didn't inventory the barn," I said. "Most everything in here is outdated or broken. Mostly used for parts or storage." I hadn't even considered inventorying the barn. I came in so infrequently that I wasn't sure what was in here.

"Why not?" asked Gray. "Especially after you found someone living in here. Did you forget?"

I don't know whether it was her manner or her tone, but I got the impression that she didn't think I was very good at my job. I swallowed my first, nasty answer and replied in an even voice. "No, nothing here is of any value. The contents of the barn are never inventoried. Did you find something from the barn on Milford?" I'd already forgotten his first name.

"No." Gray shifted some papers. "We'd like to talk to you more about this. Can we go into the office?"

I walked around the barn again, just to show Gray how thorough I could be. There, tucked behind the door, were the missing equipment and an archive box. "How did these get here?" I asked.

Troopers Gray and Bachelor came to stand beside me. "We searched the barn at least twice. They weren't here the day Grace died," said Trooper Gray.

Both Gray and Bachelor looked at me. "That means someone put the items in the barn after we searched," said Bachelor. "Who had access?"

"We got a locksmith out here the next day," I said. "It had to be in the hours between the murder and the locksmith. Less than a day."

"We didn't think to secure the barn after the investigative team left, except to lock it. We were concentrating on the crime scene." She looked at me. "Who came into the barn the next day?"

I scanned through the list of employees. "Irene called the locksmith, and he and his employees changed the lock. I've been checking the lock regularly since then." I hesitated. "I don't like the thought of somebody else being here. I haven't noticed anybody around over the last few days and there is only one key to the barn, kept in the office."

"We did a thorough search and the items weren't here when we left, the day of the murder," said Bachelor. "Who had keys to the barn before the locks were changed?"

"Irene, Kevin, and me," I said. "And there was a spare key left in the office."

"We need to know who returned the items to the barn," said Gray. "And why."

I went to open the archive box. Gray stopped me, put on a pair of gloves, and opened the box herself. Though I didn't have the list of missing items with me, it looked like most of the documents I'd put on the insurance list were here. I told the troopers that.

"You filed a claim on the missing items," said Gray. "That's insurance fraud."

"I didn't know the items were here," I said. "And I'd be pretty stupid to leave them on the premises after I filed the claim."

"Leave them there for now," said Gray. "I'll get the tech people over here to determine what's there and see if they can get fingerprints or trace evidence off them. We need to leave the barn."

We walked over to the church and I unlocked the door without any issues with the alarm. I got water from the kitchen and we sat at the conference table in the basement.

Gray started the questioning. "Has anybody been around the museum lately, someone you haven't seen before?"

"We are opening next week, so there have been cleaners and landscape people around. I don't know all of them, but I haven't seen anyone that seems out of place. I told you about the visit from Armand and his son. They showed up asking for Grace."

"Anyone else?" This from Bachelor.

"I haven't noticed anyone else," I said. "You have the threatening note that I got. It was left on my car, so it must be someone who knows me and knows where I go."

"Like Kevin Angetti?" asked Gray.

"Or like the guy Milford, who seemed to be living here." Damn, why couldn't I remember his first name? They needed to get off blaming Kevin, who was just a kid.

They asked more questions about Kevin and about the running of the museum. Then they went on to my enemies, of which there were few. Some disgruntled patrons who arrived when the museum was closed and my ex-husband's family, but nobody who would hold a grudge. My head was pounding and my back ached.

I heard boots coming down the stairs and Todd opened the door without knocking. "Am I interrupting something?" It seemed obvious that he knew he was. "I need to take Emma to her doctor's appointment."

"We were just finishing up," said Gray.

"Any updates?" I expected Todd to take out his notebook, but he refrained from doing so.

"Got an ID on the fingerprint in the barn," said Gray. "Steven Milford. Do you know him?"

Todd surprised me by answering promptly. "Yeah, local kid. Parents kicked him out of the house when he turned eighteen. Sleeps rough."

"Did you know he was sleeping in the barn here?"

"No." Todd turned to me. "Did you know?"

"I've never heard of the kid," I said. "The name meant nothing to me."

I listened while the three of them discussed Steven Milford. Suspicion of drugs, didn't get along with his stepfather, took odd jobs around the community. Unfortunately, in a small town with few employment opportunities, this wasn't an unusual event. They told Todd about finding the missing items, but refused to speculate on how they got back into the barn.

Todd once again stated that I needed to get to my appointment, and we left.

CHAPTER TWENTY-SIX

We arrived early for the appointment but were taken right in. The medical technician came in to take my blood pressure and make some notes, said the doctor would be in soon, and left us alone.

"Are we going to the Down support group?" asked Todd.

"I don't know what *we're* doing," I said, "but I don't have the time or the energy to do it right now. I'd rather wait, see how the baby is, and then see what happens."

"Why are you angry with me? I'm here at the appointment, I'm trying to help."

I really didn't want to have this conversation here and now, but I felt that I had to answer. "I want to know that you welcome this child and will be there for us. I don't want you to just help out. I want somebody who is committed to me and to the baby. I want to get married and be a family."

Todd opened his mouth to say something and his mobile phone buzzed. He looked down at the display. "It's the dispatcher. I need to talk to her." He pressed his hand to the phone and said "Mitchell here." Some buzzing on the line, followed by some "yes" and "no" answers from Todd. As we were sitting next to each other, I also heard some other words, including "fall" and "immediately."

"We'll continue this discussion later." Todd put his phone in his pocket. "We need to go."

I tried to suppress the irritation in my voice. "I'll see you at home, later."

"It's Betsy Adams. She's dead," said Todd. "You may want to come with me."

The house looked peaceful, with the flowers on the porch in full bloom. Of course, the ambulance parked in the driveway indicated something was seriously wrong. The attendants were putting a gurney into the back; I recognized Katie, the attendant who came to the historical society when Grace died. They did not seem to be in a hurry; time would do nothing for Betsy now.

On the way over, Todd told me about his conversation with Gretchen. Betsy got up in the middle of the night, fell, and hit her head on the corner of a bureau. As it was an unattended death, and Betsy was not under a doctor's care on a regular basis, the police and the medical examiner were called. Todd needed to check out the scene and I needed to talk to Gretchen, who had lost both her daughter and her mother within a few weeks of each other.

Gretchen came out of the house as we parked in front. She wore gray sweatpants and a tie-dyed T-shirt and her hair looked like it could use a good wash. "I thought Mom was just sleeping late. She does that sometimes." Gretchen pushed her hair off her face. "I didn't want to disturb her. But, when she didn't appear until almost lunch, I went in looking for her. Maybe if I'd looked sooner, she would still be alive."

"No, ma'am." This from Katie. "She died within a few minutes, probably late last night. There was nothing you could've done."

Gretchen started to cry. She cried so hard she had problems catching her breath. I put my arm around her and led her to the house. I suggested tea and she nodded. I sat Gretchen at the table and started making tea. I opened and closed several cabinets before she started giving me directions about where to find what I needed. The sobbing stopped as she continued talking.

I put both mugs on the table and sat down across from Gretchen. We sat silently as we added cream and sugar. Or rather, Gretchen did. I like mine with lemon, but didn't find any in the house.

"Mother got up in the middle of the night," said Gretchen. "I told her not to do that, not without letting me know. She has a bell in her room, to let me know when she's up."

"Maybe she didn't want to bother you." It sounded feeble, even as I said it. "Or maybe she was disoriented and didn't know what she was doing."

Gretchen took her teabag out of the mug and laid it on a napkin. "She was always so vital, so in tune with what was going on. But, recently, she started getting confused about dates and what happened when, especially at night. I think Grace's death hit her hard. She kept getting mixed up about what happened to me, what happened to her, and what happened to Grace."

"Confused, how?" I thought that maybe Todd needed to hear this, but he was still outside with the EMTs. I didn't want Gretchen to stop talking.

"She kept talking about babies, about how it was so hard having babies. But she'd get dates confused. She was just thirteen years old when she had me. Said girls matured earlier back then, but it was still hard. She wasn't married. Being a single mother couldn't have been easy. But she met my dad when she was seventeen and they were married over sixty years."

"Edwin wasn't your biological father?"

"No," said Gretchen. "We don't talk about it much, but I've known since I was eighteen that I was adopted. Back in the day, it was advised to wait until the child was an adult to tell them. Mom showed me both my birth certificates then. But Mom was confused about me. She kept talking about my baby being adopted, though I was married and living with my husband when Grace was born. Grace has always lived with me."

"Maybe she just got the two of you confused. I know my mother often called me by my sister's name."

"Maybe," she continued. "But she got up in the middle of the night to get letters written about my birth. I found these on the floor near where she collapsed." Gretchen brought out several letters on yellowing paper. "My mother kept these letters all these years. She just recently talked about that time in her life."

I took them from her and looked them over. A letter from Betsy's sister, Rachel, to her friend, saying her family was having a hard time and she was going to work in a factory in Athol. I'd seen that one before. A letter back from her friend, talking about Rachel losing a child. A nasty letter from Betsy's father, accusing her of being "wanton," and a final letter from Rachel to Betsy. "What do these letters mean? They talk about people I haven't heard of before." They painted a picture of Francis Bauman, Betsy's father, as vile and vindictive. Very different from the beleaguered valley family I had read about. But I was learning that history often got things wrong. I wondered what my children would say about me.

"Yeah, they came as a surprise to me too." Gretchen pushed her mug toward me. "Could I have some more tea?"

As I got up to pour, Gretchen continued talking.

"Grace found some letters in Mother's stuff. She was always poking around in old letters and photo albums, bringing home random things she found. Of course, I knew some of the history. Anybody who can read a birth certificate knows Mom was just thirteen when she had me. I guess I imagined some affair with a local boy, Mom being madly in love, and deciding to keep me because she loved me so much."

I sat down at the table with the refilled mugs. "I'm sure your mother loved you very much. You can tell by how she talked about you and cared for you."

Gretchen poured sugar into her tea. "Oh, I know." She stirred, clacking the spoon against the mug. "I just didn't know all the awful details of my birth."

We both turned when the door opened. Todd entered the room and looked around. "The EMTs got called out. Betsy went with them."

Gretchen started crying again. She went to the cabinet and got a box of tissues. "Guess I'm going to be needing these. I can't stop crying."

"That's a natural reaction." Todd sat down at the table with us. "Is there anything Emma or I can do to help you?"

Gretchen shook her head and took another tissue.

A scratching noise at the back door. Gretchen stood up. "I guess I need to let the dogs in," she said. "Nobody else to take care of them now." She went to the door and opened it. Prescott, the full-sized dog, led the way in, followed by Dana and Enfield. Gretchen got three bowls off the floor and filled them with kibble. "Guess they're as confused as I am. Can't think of anything to do but feed them." She put the bowls on the floor. She went to a hutch in the dining room and returned with a handful of papers.

"Do you want us to call anybody?" asked Todd. "Is there a friend you want to come stay with you?"

Gretchen shook her head. "No, I just want to be alone with my thoughts. Just before she died, Mom got out some old letters. I need to look them over. Not sure if I want to donate them to the historical society or to burn them." Gretchen turned over the documents in front of her.

My archivist training kicked in. "Don't burn them. They may be valuable records of the time before the Quabbin Reservoir."

Gretchen looked at me and shook her head. "Let me think about it. I guess what's in the letters can't hurt anyone now. I'm the only one left." She took another tissue from the box. "I know some of the history, but seeing it written down makes me sad and angry and a whole lot of things I don't have names for."

"Do you want to talk about the letters?" I realized that, while they were historical documents to me, they were personal to this family. "Unless you'd prefer to do it at another time."

"No, I don't have anything planned for the next few hours," said Gretchen. "I don't even have to take care of Mom or wonder where Grace is." She took a deep breath, but she didn't cry. Prescott came over and sat down beside her. She patted his head. "Guess I have to take care of you guys, though." Prescott put his head in her lap. We all stared at the letters on the table.

"When my aunt, Alma, died, my grandparents were devastated. My grandmother stayed in her room most of the day and granddad started drinking. Rachel was the one who had to look after Betsy, my mother, though she was only sixteen herself." Gretchen smiled. "Betsy was three years old, but she was already a terror. Rachel took her everywhere with her. I guess they were happier being out of the house."

Gretchen turned each of the pages over, one at a time. "The letters written by Rachel are sad, but the ones that come later are worse. When she was eighteen, she left the home permanently and took a job in a factory in Athol. Betsy was just five, and she moved with the family to Pelham. Her mother put her into school a year early; my mother always thought it was because she couldn't deal with her."

"It must have been awful for Betsy, to think that she wasn't wanted," I said. "To carry that burden."

Gretchen stroked Prescott's head. The other two dogs came over and lay at her feet. "The burden got heavier. Rachel had a hard time adjusting to her new life. She took up with a lot of local men and got pregnant several times. Most of the babies died before they were born or shortly afterward. Her father was drinking a lot and blamed her for the family's downfall. He ended up in the Worcester Lunatic Asylum, where he wrote this nasty letter."

Gretchen slid the letter over, to land in front of me. It was a nasty letter. Rachel's father accused her of putting him in the asylum and of being wanton. It hurt me, and I wasn't the object of his wrath.

"He talks about Betsy being a problem, too," I said. "What did she do?"

"She got pregnant too. Had me when she was still a child." Gretchen took the letter back and stared at it. "Never had another child. I often wondered about that." Gretchen put the letter down. "I'm not wondering any more. After he got released, my grandfather filed a petition on his wanton daughters and both were sterilized by the state. My mother said she didn't know it would mean she'd never have another child."

I didn't know what to say, so I said nothing. I reached across and took Gretchen's hand. She was crying again.

"How could my grandfather be so cruel? When my mother married Edwin Adams, the man I consider my father, she told me I would have a brother or a sister. I kept asking her when the baby would arrive, years after she must have figured out what happened."

"I'm so sorry," I said. "But it must have been a relief for your mother to talk about it."

Gretchen removed her hand from mine. "She did seem to find some peace, at the end. But I still have to go through the rest of her belongings. Don't know what other awful things I might find."

"I will help you, if you want me to." I was afraid that she might destroy some valuable records because of her grief, but my main concern was her misery.

"No," she said. "I have to do it. My mother would want me to."

I heard Todd shift in his chair. "Can I get you something? Coffee or tea? I know it's not what you need, but can I get you anything?" He looked at the empty mugs in front of us. "Guess you don't need any more tea."

Gretchen wiped her face. "No, it's just painful to talk about. And I miss my mother."

Todd's radio crackled and he left the room. He was wanted at the scene of a car accident. I stayed with Gretchen. We didn't talk much, just sat and patted the dogs.

Miss Louisa Ames
Pelham, Massachusetts

July 20, 1940
Dear Rachel,

My mother says that I should not write to you but we've been friends for almost twenty years. I can't imagine the pain you are going through. When you came to my wedding last year, with Frederick, we talked about getting married and having our children together.

Stephen and I have been blessed with a son, Stephen, Jr., and you have lost your child. My sympathy goes out to you.

July 28, 1940

My mother just told me that Frederick has gone missing and you are alone. He is your natural husband and I know you miss him greatly. Perhaps we can meet soon when circumstances are more favorable. Until then, I will pray for you and your child in Heaven.

Love always,
Louisa

WORCESTER LUNATIC ASYLUM
WORCESTER, MASSACHUSETTS

September 6, 1942
Dear Elizabeth,

I am writing this as your father, to protect and guide you, though you are no daughter to me. When I needed help, after Alma's death, you went on to school without a thought to me. Many a night I did not eat because you would not return home and feed me. Because you would not take care of me, I have been declared a public nuisance and a lunatic and have ended up in this asylum, where I am not allowed to go anywhere unattended and the food is inedible. Destroy this letter after you have read it, as you and I will have no further communication.

A demon has possessed you and our home. Your lies and perversions have put me in this horrible place. You are no better than your sister, pregnant for the fourth time, by three different men. God has seen fit to punish her by seeing that each of her children die shortly after birth. Except for the latest one, who is three months old but sickly and barely hanging on.

The war may get me out of this hell of a place. They need factory workers, even crazy ones. Not that I'm crazy. This world is not right, there are too many people being born who cannot live up to their potential. In the valley, I was a farmer and we had enough to eat. Then the demons took our land and my lovely daughter, Alma. The government set out to take away everything that was precious to me.

You put me into this horrible place, with your lies about my drinking and my cruelty. And the wicked demon of your lust. Though you are prone to wanton conduct, like your sister, you dare to accuse me of fathering your child. I have only tried to protect and guide you. I do not know why I have such ungrateful offspring. Though you are only thirteen years old, you have learned the wanton ways of your sister.

Damnation on both of you.

June 18, 1946
Dear Betsy,

Papa is looking for you. He has been released from his confinement and is working at a local factory. He and the factory owner, Mr. Styles, have become fast friends and continue to wreak havoc in my life. Please forgive me. I know I have made a wreck of my life but I did not mean to bring you into my wretchedness.

Papa and Mr. Styles have succeeded in taking Doris from me. After three lost children, I was so happy to have Doris survive after her first birthday, though she was sickly and cried constantly. She was my child, the proof of my love for Lorenzo. Then Lorenzo was killed in some place called Morocco, where he went to be a soldier.

Papa and Mr. Styles said they found a good home for Doris. But they would not tell me where she was. And they threatened to put me into a home for the feebleminded and wanton. My only hope for freedom was to submit to an operation. I consented.

It was not until the operation was over that they told me I could not have any more children. And I did not know where Doris was. I missed Lorenzo so much. He would have known what to do.

Last week, they brought me before the Board of Social Hygiene again and asked me questions about you. I learned for the first time that you have a daughter too and she is named Gretchen, after our mother. And, as the Board of Social Hygiene has determined that feeblemindedness and wantonness are hereditary, they made you submit to the same operation.

But, thank God, I learned that you are more clever than I am. You escaped, with your soldier husband and the baby, and the Board doesn't know where you are. They questioned me for hours about your habits, your life, and where you might be. As we have had little contact over the last years, I was unable (and unwilling) to give them information.

I hope you are safe and with Gretchen, wherever you are. Please forgive me.

*Love always,
Rachel*

CHAPTER TWENTY-SEVEN

The phone was ringing when we got home. Nobody ever calls on the house phone and I don't know why we keep paying the bill. I'd ordered the phone years ago when there was no mobile service at the house or in most of New Salem. Probably a telemarketer. I looked at Todd, who shrugged. I let it ring.

The voicemail still worked and someone was leaving a message. "Emma, hi. It's Hadley. I'd like to talk to you. Sorry I left your house in a hurry last month, but I need to ask you a question."

I picked up the phone. "Hadley, I'm glad to hear from you. I was worried about you and the kids. What's going on?"

Silence, for what seemed like a long time. Probably thirty seconds. "Well, I'm confused. The kids were so happy to be back home, to see their stuff. I shouldn't complain. It's nice to hear a friendly voice."

I realized how little I knew about my sister. The years of estrangement loomed over us. I wasn't sure I knew the present-day Hadley at all. She was my sister, but she seemed more than confused. "You said you had a question for me. What is it?"

More silence. "I forgot what I meant. Hold on a minute." Kid noises in the background, instructions to play in the other room. "I've got to go. The kids need me." She hung up.

Todd entered the room with Barney on a leash. "What was that about?"

I shook my head. "I don't know. It was Hadley, said she had to ask me a question. Then she hung up."

"I know she's your sister, but I don't think you should invite her over here again. I just got the pink goop out of the carpet. Had to keep the door closed, so Barney wouldn't eat it."

"She sounded strange," I said. "She talked about how much the kids liked being back home, though she left here a few weeks ago. And she was in a hurry to go. I wonder if Jim told her to hang up."

Todd sat down at the table and Barney sat on the floor. "What can we do to help? Well, Barney's probably not going to be a great help, but what can I do?"

This is why I stick with Todd. If you can define the problem, he's there to solve it. It's the messy problems that are an issue. That reminded me, we hadn't finished our conversation from the doctor's office. "Can I go with you and Barney for your walk?" It would give us a chance to talk with fewer interruptions.

"Of course." Todd and Barney stood up. "You're always welcome." I grabbed a water bottle and my phone and we left.

We walked down the road, with the buds now visible on the trees. Most times in late spring and early summer, I am sneezing and my nose runs. Maybe a benefit of pregnancy was that it took care of my allergies. Not that I wanted to make it a permanent solution. Now that we were out in nature, and relaxed, I was reluctant to bring up the topic of commitment and marriage again, though I realized it needed to be discussed. Todd must have been thinking about our talk earlier in the day, also.

"We'll have to reschedule your appointment with Dr. Nancy," he said. "Maybe we can do that when we get home."

"It'll be too late, the office will be closed. And I don't have my schedule, so we can't do it here." He'd brought up the topic, so I went on. "Maybe we should finish the conversation we had in the office."

"Maybe," he said. We walked for a few more minutes, and I though he was avoiding the topic. Then he spoke again. "I could see myself spending the rest of my life walking the dog with you. And then bringing the baby along."

This was a start. "Life is more than taking walks with the baby and me." I turned to face him. "What if our child has special needs? What if he needs more care than the average child?"

"Then we'll take care of him." Barney pulled Todd to the side of the road and he walked away from me. They explored the bushes and the broken twigs on the ground; then Barney did his business. They rejoined me on the path, and we continued to walk in silence.

"I want to be with you, and I want to take care of the baby," said Todd. "After this dustup with Brian and Dierdre, I realized that being a father means sticking by your kids, no matter what. So that's what I'm going to do."

"I know you may not understand this, but that's not enough." I went on to explain about wanting to be with me, not just staying with the family as an obligation. I didn't see marriage as the ceremony, but as the commitment to each other. We could get married at the town hall, as long as I thought that Todd was in it because he wanted to be.

"I already have one failed marriage," said Todd. "I don't want to have another one. There's the age difference; the fact that we'll be retiring when this child is in college, if he ever gets to college. If not, we may be caring for him until we die. It's a lot to think about."

"I'll raise this kid by myself if I have to. This is probably my last chance at motherhood, and I'm going to take it. I have a failed marriage too, probably more violent than yours. But I see it as a learning experience, so I can do it better next time."

"There is that," said Todd. "Is it enough to say that I can't imagine a future without you and the baby in it?"

"Yeah," I said. "It's enough."

"I think this calls for a token of our new commitment. I'm going to start looking for engagement rings." Todd looked at me. "If that's okay with you."

"It's wonderful," I said.

"And I know," said Todd. "No diamonds."

When we got home, there was another note on my car: "Stop asking about Grace & Betsy. You'll be sorry."

CHAPTER TWENTY-EIGHT

The next day, I gave the note to Trooper Bachelor. He didn't have any questions this time; he just took it, preserved in a plastic sleeve. I'd made a copy of it before I turned it over. Then I went to the post office to mail some packages and I took the trash to the dump.

The house phone was ringing when I got home, same as yesterday. I recognized the number, same as yesterday.

"Hello, Hadley."

"Emma, I'm so glad you're home. I need somebody to talk to." And who better than a sister?

"Did you remember the question that you needed to ask me?" I tried not to sound annoyed, but my feet were swollen and my head hurt.

No hesitation this time. "He hit Merry. I need to do something."

"Is Merry safe? Does she need medical attention?" I felt the heat rise from my feet to my head. Didn't do anything for my headache, but it helped me focus. All my issues with injured and dead children flashed through my mind. Why hadn't I done something yesterday?

"No, she's fine. He just slapped her. He's gone now. Said he had to clear his head."

It didn't sound like it was fine, and he could always come back. I heard Merry crying in the background. "What do you need from me?"

"She's crying again," said Hadley. "I'll call you back."

I sat at the kitchen bar, trying to think. I wasn't going to do nothing this time. Tried to call Todd but he was at work and his phone was off. It wasn't an emergency, so I didn't want to pull him from his job. But I needed to do something. I suppressed the urge to go to Hadley's house and make it an emergency. But there was something I could do. I called the local women's center and got current information about the services and shelter beds. I went on their website and got a "domestic emergency" checklist. Marked the information to send to Hadley, should she ask. After forty-five minutes, an energy bar, and a cup of tea, the phone rang. I picked it up and told Hadley I was glad she called me back.

"I wasn't going to call you back," she said. "I don't think there's anything you can do. But it might be nice to talk to someone. Can I come over and see you?"

"No." I immediately felt as if I'd let her down. I felt like the bad sister. Then I thought of what had happened the last time, with Jim assaulting me, and I wondered whether I should have pressed charges. But that meant that Jim would've been arrested and Todd would have taken him to a town with a jail. And, given the vagaries of release and bail, Jim would probably have been back in town before Todd. But that was the past, and I needed to protect myself now. "I'm pregnant and I don't want Jim around here when he's angry."

"He's only a problem when he's been drinking," said Hadley. "And he's not at home right now."

Which meant he could be out drinking. I refrained from pointing that out to her. "Why did you call me? Did you remember your question?"

"I need to leave the house. I thought I'd do it while Jim wasn't angry." I heard the sounds of running water and a chopping knife. "I'm making food now, but I'll leave as soon as I feed the kids. I can't take the car; that would make Jim angry. Can you come and get me?"

I was glad that she was leaving Jim, but it didn't sound like she had much of a plan. Fortunately, I'd done my research. "Hadley, between phone calls, I talked to the people at the women's shelter. If you call them, they can meet you and help you get to a safe place."

"Women's shelter?" Hadley sounded like I'd suggested she go to a bordello. "If Jim knows I'm there, he'll be very upset."

Jim got upset at everything; that was the problem. Again, I didn't think it'd be useful to point that out to Hadley. We made arrangements for her to call and to get out of the house. I agreed to meet her, after she and the children were settled in the shelter. I had my doubts that she would be there, but I agreed.

CHAPTER TWENTY-NINE

Hadley did go to the shelter. It took some doing, but we managed it. She left the house, with the kids, and two duffel bags. Jim cooperated by staying away. She walked to the middle of town and stood on one of the two corners with a stoplight. Someone from the women's shelter picked her up and brought her to their office, where I met her. Even though I was living with the police chief, the staff was reluctant to tell me where the shelter was. It was one of the poorest kept secrets in the county, because of the number of police calls to the address, but I respected their wishes. I just hoped that I hadn't made a mistake and Hadley wouldn't be one of those women who asked their partners to pick them up outside the shelter.

We sat in a dingy room, with two desks and four chairs. A bulletin board was covered with schedules and chore charts and other things necessary to run a house with multiple families. All four chairs were occupied by Hadley, me, Mary, who had come to pick up Hadley, and Bea, with a paper triangle on her desk that identified her as the intake coordinator. It was after nine when we got there, so the kids were sleeping in another room.

"I'm not sure I want to do this." Hadley twisted her wedding ring around her finger and looked around the room. "The kids may not want to stay here."

"We understand that," said Bea. "We try to impress on the children the importance of secrecy, but some contact their other parent anyway."

"That's Garrett. He made a mess when we stayed at Emma's house."

Bea turned to me. "And you are Emma? How did you come to be here?"

All eyes turned to me. How did I describe my involvement? Hadley needed a friend, and I tried to help her. "Hadley was in a car accident," I said. "My partner, the police chief, and I got her help. She's my sister, but I hadn't seen her in a long time before the accident. A few days later, she came to my house and asked for help. Her husband, Jim, followed her there and pushed me down. My partner, the police chief, drove him home and I stayed with Hadley." I realized the narrative was incomplete.

"Why wasn't he arrested?" This question came from Mary. "I understand that Hadley had bruises on her wrists."

Hadley sat silently, not helping at all.

"I asked him not to." Might as well get the tough stuff out of the way. "We live in New Salem, without a jail or even a police station. Todd would've had to take Mr. Mason two towns over, to the nearest processing facility. Given the amount of paperwork involved, and the bail guidelines, Mason could have been home before Todd. I didn't want to chance that."

The explanation sounded convoluted, even as I said it. But these women, in a city with a full-time police force, didn't understand the pressures of a single officer. I knew Todd did it because I asked, and I still believed it was the right thing to do, but it didn't follow protocol.

"Don't you think that Hadley, the person with the bruises, should have made the decision about an arrest?" asked Bea. "She needs to be empowered in this situation."

"I didn't want Jim arrested," said Hadley. "I just wanted some time to think."

"Okay, let's do the intake," said Bea. She went on to gather biographical information on Hadley and her children. Hadley had medical insurance cards and a checkbook, in both her and her husband's names, but she did not have birth certificates, social security cards, or any of the other requirements to get financial assistance. Bea made an ever increasing list of things that needed to be obtained or looked into if Hadley was going to stay in the shelter. This seemed to go on forever, but finally Bea got to the matter at hand.

"What brought you here tonight?" she asked.

"I don't know." Hadley continued to play with her wedding ring and look around the room. This was followed by several minutes of silence, occasionally broken by Hadley's sighs.

"Do you plan to stay at the shelter?" That was the next question Bea asked.

"I think so. The kids are already asleep. I might as well stay." Hadley sounded like she was trying to convince herself that it was a good plan. "I can't stay with my sister."

Again, I felt like the bad sister. My reason told me that we were both in danger at my house, but my heart said that I should have done more to support and help my sister.

"What do you hope to get out of your stay at the shelter?" asked Mary. I'd forgotten she was in the room, in the chair in the corner.

"I don't know. I'm so confused. Maybe things will be clearer." Hadley looked from one to the other of us, as if we had the answers for her. "I just want my family to be safe."

"That's important," said Bea. "Why do you think your family is not safe?"

"He hit Merry." Hadley's voice was barely audible. "He didn't mean to, he was swiping things off the counter and he hit her."

"How did that happen?" Bea was an expert at asking open-ended questions. And she sounded like she was just interested in the details, not judging. I wished I possessed that skill. Right now, I wanted to shake Hadley and get the story out of her. But I controlled myself because I knew that probably wouldn't get us what we needed.

"He was swiping things off the counter, you know, with a backhand motion." Hadley demonstrated on the desktop. "And when his hand came back, he hit Merry. Her lip bled."

"Why was he swiping things off the counter? Was he cleaning it?" asked Bea.

"No." Hadley paused for what seemed like a long time, but was probably only a few seconds. "He said it was dirty, I hadn't picked up things. The plate broke and that's what cut Merry's lip. I told him to stop but he wouldn't." Another, longer pause. "Maybe I should stay here tonight."

Mary got up and offered to take Hadley to her kids and get her settled for the night. They picked up the duffel bags on the floor and left.

"Do you think she'll stay for more than the night?" Hadley seemed reluctant to even say anything bad about Jim, so I asked the question.

"Some do, some don't. It's not my position to judge. I just help them until they're finally ready to leave." Bea took the forms that she had filled out and placed them in a file folder. "I'll put them in the computer tomorrow. Is there anything else?"

"No, it just all seems so pointless. She left him once, came to my house, and went back before the night was even through. I thought, this time, I'd get her to a shelter and things would be different."

Bea sighed. "I used to work with the police department. Domestic violence specialist. I quit." She sounded like she expected me to say something, but I didn't have a response. "You only see these women when they're at their worst. With bruises, being called names, and scared for their children. You separate them from the abuser, sometimes arrest him. It's almost always a him. Give the woman information and then you do the whole thing over again in a few weeks. You know about the cycle of violence?"

"Yeah," I said. "There's a blowup, the abuser apologizes and is on their best behavior for a few weeks and everything is fine. The tension increases, there is another explosion, and then the best behavior again."

"Not exactly right, but close enough." Bea pushed some literature and pamphlets across the table to me. "It's the best behavior part that makes them keep going back. But it's exhausting for everyone involved. At least here, I can occasionally see a success story. With the police, it's just an endless cycle. But you live with a cop, you know this."

I thought I knew about the difficulties of policing, but I'd never thought of it this way. Todd saw people in the worst situations, every day, and he never knew whether they made it out or not. Tough way to live.

"Yes, and I need to get home to the cop. Tell him that I'm glad he goes out every day and does his job." I picked up my things and left.

CHAPTER THIRTY

Another memorial service at the historical society. This one even more complicated than the last, because Betsy was one of the last surviving inhabitants of the Swift River Valley. All the other survivors wanted to attend, which meant getting hearing assistance devices and rearranging furniture to accommodate wheelchairs. We'd had a handicap ramp installed when the church was moved, back in 1985. We removed some pews and exhibits to accommodate the crowd.

Betsy had left instructions for her funeral, down to the pictures to display and the hymns to sing. The minister actually knew her, from her years as a trustee of the church. She also asked that her granddaughter, Grace, speak at her service. Guess she didn't anticipate outliving her grandchild. This time, Gretchen sat in the wooden chair at the front of the church. Beside her was Armand LaValley, holding her hand and whispering to her. Gretchen had said that they dated in high school and it looked like they might be trying to have a second chance together.

Irene had done most of the coordination of this service, leaving me to my duties, now that the historical society was open. I scheduled docents for this service also. The Whitaker-Clary House was not handicap accessible, but most of the people who showed up wanted to see other parts of the museum. Some folks with canes and walkers wandered outside, looking at the guideboards that used to stand in the valley, showing directions and miles to towns no longer in existence.

Jesse came into the church and started looking at the flowers around the sanctuary. There were a dozen bouquets spread around the church. He stopped at a large display in a wide vase, with roses and lily of the valley. He picked up the card, read it, and walked over to Gretchen and Armand with it.

"They messed up the card," he said. "I told them that it should be Armand and Son with an ampersand. They put in an 'and' instead. I told them."

"It's not important," said Armand. "It's just important that we sent her flowers."

"But it is important," said Jesse. "When we repainted the truck, she said we needed an ampersand. And it's not there."

I started toward them, before this escalated into an incident such as the one at Grace's services. Armand took Jesse aside and spoke to him in the corner. Jesse calmed down, returned the card to the flowers, and sat in one of the pews. I sat in the back of the church.

The service began with a prayer and a hymn. The minister talked about Betsy as a child. He did remark that he wasn't that old, but Betsy had talked about her childhood in the valley on many occasions. He talked about her work with the church and her love of the Swift River Valley Historical Society. He told a funny story about Betsy insisting that the church furnace was making funny noises, right up until the day it stopped working and she was vindicated. Then Irene spoke and some members of her church spoke. Jesse, who was there with Armand, remained silent through the service.

Afterward, we all went downstairs for the spread, courtesy of the church ladies. Todd came in the door just as I headed down. He apologized for his being late, but said he was held up at work.

I grabbed a sandwich, as I always seemed to be hungry these days. Armand was standing alone in the corner, so I went up to talk to him.

"Looks like you and Gretchen are getting along well," I said.

"Yeah, we're talking," he said. "Don't know where it will go. Can I get you something to drink?"

"No, I'm good." Was it me or did everyone feel the need to feed and water the pregnant lady?

Todd joined us and handed me a bottle of water. "Thought you might need this." I took it, though it made holding the plate and the sandwich more difficult. "How are you doing, Armand?"

"Okay. Wish I didn't have to come to two memorial services within a few weeks."

"Yeah, it's tough," said Todd. "Hey, Armand, do you know anything about notes being left on Emma's car?"

He furrowed his brow. "What kind of notes?"

"Threatening notes," said Todd.

Armand was silent for several seconds. "Why would I know about threatening notes?"

"Well, if you had something shady going with Grace, you may not want anyone to know about it." Todd stared at Armand.

"This is a fine place to bring this up. We just buried Betsy." Armand's voice got lower, he shook his head, and he seemed genuinely upset.

"You seem to avoid me everywhere else I try to talk to you." Todd took my arm. "But if you're that upset, we'll leave." Todd led me outside.

"What was that about?" I asked. "Did you find his prints on the note?"

"No," said Todd. "No fingerprints. He just seemed to be the person with the biggest grudge against you." We started walking toward the car. "But he didn't seem to know anything about the notes."

OBITUARY

Elizabeth Grace (Bauman) Adams

Elizabeth Grace (Bauman) Adams died on June 20 of this year. She was born and spent her early childhood in Enfield, Massachusetts in the Swift River Valley, before it was flooded to become the Quabbin Reservoir She devoted a significant portion of her adult life to the Swift River Valley Historical Society, dedicated to saving the memorabilia and artifacts left behind by those forced to leave their homes. Elizabeth spent her entire adult life in New Salem, Massachusetts, so that she could be near her beloved Swift River and her ancestors.

In addition to her love of history and the museum, Elizabeth, called "Betsy" by her friends, was dedicated to her family. She is the daughter of Gretchen (Atkins) and Francis Bauman and was predeceased by her sisters, Alma and Rachel. She lived, until her death, with her daughter, Gretchen (Adams) Connelly. Her granddaughter and a namesake, Grace Elizabeth Connelly, died earlier this year.

A celebration of her life will be held on June 30 at the Swift River Valley Historical Society in New Salem. In lieu of flowers, donations may be made to the historical society.

July

CHAPTER THIRTY-ONE

It was time to go see Dr. Nancy again. This time I had a list of questions for her, and lists of resources I had discovered on the internet. I wanted answers and her opinion about where to go for reliable information. For some reason, I hadn't applied my list-making to my pregnancy. That changed today.

Todd was already out of bed and taking a shower. It was only seven thirty and it was already above eighty degrees. Next time, I'd plan to be pregnant in the winter. Of course, that meant the risk of slipping on ice and falling down with my swollen body, but this heat torture wasn't good either. Then I realized I was thinking about another child. Time to concentrate on the one that was coming.

"You going to get out of bed today?" asked Todd. He came out of the shower wearing only a towel, and he looked good. "Shall I take you to the doctor in your pajamas?"

I climbed out of bed and found one of my two clean outfits that still went around my belly. It was July, so the shoe problem was solved by sandals. I tucked the list of questions into my purse, went downstairs to join Todd, and was ready to go.

"Aren't you going to eat?" asked Todd. "I made coffee."

"I'm not hungry," I said. I wasn't about to throw up on my clean clothes.

"You need to eat." Todd popped two slices of bread into the toaster.

"Maybe just coffee and toast." I sat down at the table. "Do you have a list of questions for the doctor?"

"No." Todd shook his head. "I thought I'd wait until we were closer to your due date, so the doctor would know more about what to expect." He slathered jam on his toast. "Do you have a list?" He smiled, as I always have a list.

"Yup. Questions about dry skin and stretch marks and what to do when the baby's sitting on my bladder. Questions about swollen feet and when this morning sickness is actually going to stop."

Todd reached across to take my hand. "I know this is tough on you, but I'm here to help. It's been a while for me so you have to tell me what you need."

"Can you do anything about swollen feet or morning sickness?"

"No, but I can make dinner so you can put your feet up and bring ice. I can make toast and whatever else you need to keep food down. I love you, Emma, and I want this to work out."

I finished my toast and stood up. "I love you too, but we've got to get going or we're going to be late."

We got into the car and started down the driveway. Todd got us out on to the main road, and I reached for my phone to plug it into the car.

"Can we talk instead?" he asked. "No music."

I put my phone into my purse. "Sure," I said. "What do you want to talk about?"

"Have you looked into the support groups for parents of Down syndrome children?"

"Yeah, I looked online. Some groups are virtual and the nearest in-person one is in Northampton. I don't want to drive that far, at night, to attend a group." I looked out the window. I'd gone to the websites that Dr. Nancy recommended, but I didn't ask for further information or sign up for the newsletter. I didn't want to explore further right now.

"I think we should try one of the online groups." Todd continued to stare out the windshield, not looking at me. "If we're going to deal with a baby with special needs, we should get all the information we can, to be prepared."

"But we won't know what we're dealing with until he's born. We can make decisions then." I'd tried to avoid this conversation. I'd had arguments with Todd because he didn't like to anticipate specific problems and he was always on guard. Now he wanted to learn more about our baby, but I wasn't ready. Would we ever be on the same wavelength? I also realized that it was unfair. We'd had four good years together and the last few months had been hard. I knew life threw curves and we could work through this together. "You're right. We should look into this."

We spent the rest of the trip in silence. Dr. Nancy was delivering a baby, so we saw another doctor. She was a tall woman with coffee-colored skin. She wore a shirt that said "U.S. Army" underneath her white coat, with a tag that said "Angela Andrew, M.D."

"Did you serve?" asked Todd. When she said yes, they spent a few minutes discussing their experiences. Dr. Andrew redirected the conversation to the pregnancy.

"You chose to continue the pregnancy," she said. "That's an unusual choice today. Very few Down syndrome babies are being born." I wanted to be angry at her, but she didn't sound judgmental, just stating facts.

"We want a child," said Todd. "And we plan to raise this one to the best of our ability." Like Dr. Andrew, Todd spoke as if he were stating facts apparent to anyone. Maybe this would all work out for the best.

"Now, Dr. Graber gave you a list of resources and support groups. Have you looked into any of them?" Dr. Andrew's military training was showing. She had a checklist and she was going through it. I liked that in a woman and a medical provider.

"We discussed that on the way over," said Todd. "We've been doing some research, but I think it's time to start talking to people who have been through the experience."

"And you, Ms. Wetherby, what do you think?"

"I think we need as much information as we can get." Surprising even myself, I found that this was true.

The rest of the appointment was taken up in making sure we had the most current literature and resources, and Dr. Andrew doing the prenatal exam. She was not talkative and supportive like Dr. Nancy, but I found I appreciated her quiet competence. If she ended up delivering my baby, I knew I'd be in good hands. I was feeling more confident and relaxed when we left the office.

CHAPTER THIRTY-TWO

We were driving home when Todd's phone rang. I didn't recognize the number that appeared on the screen.

"I've got to answer this," said Todd. "I called a number of people to reschedule and don't want to be playing phone tag." He pressed the screen and said, "Chief Mitchell."

"Hello, Chief, this is Marla at dispatch. I have a message for you."

"Go ahead."

"Just a minute, let me bring it up." I heard the sounds of a keyboard. "Bea called from the women's shelter. Wanted to tell you that Hadley Mason and her kids left the shelter. Her husband, Jim, came to pick them up and they left peacefully."

"Thanks, Marla." Todd ended the call. "Guess that was to be expected."

"I really hoped she'd stay away this time. It's so much better for her and probably for the kids also." I shook my head. "I tried to support her, to get her some help. Then she talks to Jim again, he says he'll do better, and she believes him."

"I see it all the time in my job," said Todd. "It does get discouraging. Especially in the jail, where the guys end up after they've lost it. Most of them are responsible and even funny around the other prisoners. Even around the guards. They just screw up their relationships with women."

"It's hard not to, when you think that your way is the best way for everyone." Now where had that statement come from? But Todd could be overbearing and protective. He was also committed to me and to the baby and he enabled me to work part-time at a job I loved. Full-time archivist jobs were hard to come by and, in New Salem, required a hefty commute.

"Want to go out to lunch?" Leave it to Todd to go from a profound discussion to lunch. "It's a beautiful day; we can eat outside, at the picnic tables at the general store."

I thought about my conversation with Bea and my promise to see things from Todd's perspective. A leisurely lunch and time to talk seemed to be just the thing.

We pulled into the general store and it appeared that several people had the same idea. I sat at the last open picnic table and Todd went in to get us sandwiches and soup. I'd just taken the top off my container of soup when Todd's phone rang. He answered it and looked at me. "Emma is not answering her phone," he said.

I pulled my phone from my purse. I'd turned it off in the doctor's office earlier in the day, and I didn't turn it on again. I pressed some buttons and brought up my missed messages. Three of them from Gretchen. One from a Curtis Hapgood; I ignored that one. "What was Gretchen calling me about?" I asked.

"She said that she found something we should see. Called me when she couldn't get you."

Todd and I gulped down our lunches and made our way to Gretchen's house. Now Gretchen was alone. I wondered how she was doing, surrounded by mementoes of her dead mother and daughter. And, of course, the dogs. They came running when we pulled up and jumped on us when we got out of the car. Gretchen opened the door and the dogs ran inside. We came at a slower pace.

"I'm sorry about the dogs jumping on you. Are you okay?" Gretchen was looking at me when she asked, as if my pregnancy made me more vulnerable to being knocked over. Maybe it did, I'd never considered that. I told her it wasn't a problem. We went inside and sat down at the table. Then the usual conversation about beverages; both Todd and I declined.

"What did you want to talk to us about?" Todd got right to the point. And I was glad he did. My feet were aching again.

"I was going through Grace's things and I found this paper. It's not really a legal matter and it's personal. Well, some people around here know parts of it, but we don't talk about it much." Gretchen must have been upset; I'd never heard her ramble on like this before. "But Grace was always curious, about her history and her ancestors, and she gave us these kits for Christmas."

I glanced over at Todd, who looked just as confused as I did. I thought of asking a question, but Gretchen just continued on. "I didn't want to do it, no telling what might happen. But then Grace said it was a good idea, and she was so insistent, that we agreed. I knew it could turn out bad, but I did it anyway."

"What did you do?" I didn't want to interrupt her, but I couldn't figure out what she was talking about.

Gretchen stood up. "I'm going to get coffee. Does anyone else want some?" Both Todd and I shook our heads. Gretchen went into the kitchen. She returned a few moments later with a mug and more documents. She sat back down at the table.

"It's so hard to talk about," she said. "Even after all these years." She took a long drink of coffee, stared into the mug, and continued talking. "Armand and I were an item when we were teenagers. I was so taken with him, but I also had my swimming career. Not career, I was an amateur competitor, going to be in the Olympics. You had to be an amateur, not professional pay, back then." She stopped and looked from me to Todd. "Armand and I had a child. I never saw the child, didn't even know whether it was a boy or a girl. Gave it up for adoption as soon as he was born. I know that it was a he. I know that now, I didn't know then."

"How awful that you were separated," I said. "Has the child contacted you?" If the child had contacted her, that would explain her recent knowledge of its sex.

"Not yet," said Gretchen. "He started with his father."

"He contacted Armand? When?" asked Todd.

"Actually, Armand contacted him. I'm not telling this story very well." Gretchen took another sip from her coffee cup. "Grace gave us DNA testing kits for Christmas. I didn't want to take the test, because I knew she had a sibling out there somewhere. We discussed it for months and I finally agreed, as did Betsy. I found the results in Grace's things." Gretchen took a long breath and let it out. "The baby was in the area all these years. It's Kyle Angetti, Kevin's father. Kevin is my grandson."

"Isn't that unusual? Giving a child up for adoption in the same neighborhood where it was born?" I had so many other questions going through my head. Why the hell hadn't she said something when Grace was murdered? Did this information lead to Grace's death? And why was she telling us this now? But I decided to ask this question. I guess I was a bit confused too.

"How long have you known this information?" asked Todd. Leave it to him to ask the right questions.

Gretchen smoothed out the paper in front of her. "I've only known for a few days. Armand seems to have known longer. Grace went to him before she died."

"Why didn't he tell us this? What was he trying to hide?" Todd fired questions at Gretchen. "Are you covering up for him?"

Gretchen started crying. "No. I'm telling you this because Armand thought he was protecting me. By not telling." She took a tissue out of the box on the table, wiped her eyes, and blew her nose. "I told him it wasn't fair to Grace to keep information from the police."

It seemed this family had a history of children being in a bad place. First, Betsy had Gretchen at a young age, and then Gretchen gave up her child for adoption. But it was Grace who was murdered and there still wasn't a motive or a suspect. My thoughts were going around and around in my head.

Todd didn't seem to have that problem, as he continued to ask questions. "You mean that your child was in the area for over fifty years and you never knew it? That seems a little hard to believe." Todd stopped talking, waiting for an answer from Gretchen.

"I wasn't looking for my child in town," said Gretchen. "I was told that he was adopted by a family in Maine. My mother lied to me." Gretchen wailed at those last words, but I didn't know whether it was for her child or for her mother's lies.

"How did she lie to you?" That still wasn't clear to me.

"She told me she'd found a good family for my child. Out of state. But then she talked the Angettis into taking him, so she could watch her grandchild grow up."

"How do you know all this?" I asked. With Betsy dead, it could all be speculation.

"My mother left me a letter, to be opened after she died. It gave directions for her funeral, her money and property, and told me about my son." Gretchen grabbed another handful of tissues from the box. "I wish we could have talked about it when she was alive."

"Can I see the letter?" Todd asked. His voice was softer and more gentle that before. "It might play a part in Grace's death."

"I don't think so, but I don't see any harm in it." She pushed the two pieces of paper across the table. "The top letter is the DNA tests and the letter underneath is from my mother."

Todd read the first letter and passed it on to me. It was written by Betsy, almost ten years ago. She asked for forgiveness and gave Gretchen specific instructions about where to find important documents. It did not include a combination to the safe.

"She mentions the safe, but doesn't give the combination. Do you know it? Have you looked at the contents?"

"Yeah, she always referred to the combination as 'the north thing.' It's the latitude marker for the center of the Quabbin. Or maybe it's the longitude. Forty-two, twenty-one, thirty-three. Sometimes she uses 'the west thing' for seventy-two, eighteen, double zero. That's the other geographic marker."

"And Betsy knew this?" I'd seen those numbers recently. On a paper under Grace's body.

"Always. She told me the coordinates when I was just a girl. And now, with Google, those are the numbers that come up. Handy reference if I ever need it." Gretchen reached across the table for the documents.

"I'll need to take these," said Todd. "Though I'm not sure how relevant the coordinates are."

So many secrets in this family. I guess in all families. I'd just learned my sister went back to her abusive husband. I found my eyes filling with tears.

"Do you want us to call someone to stay with you?" Todd asked.

Gretchen shook her head. "The dogs will keep me company."

GENETICS JOURNEY
20466 GENETICS DRIVE
TERRE HAUTE, IN 47805

March 12, 2023

Grace Elizabeth Connelly
450 Millington Commons
New Salem, MA 01355

RE: Genetics Journey testing
Dear Ms. Connelly:

    Thank you for interest in Genetics Journey. I hope the information you obtain assists you in your quest for more information about your family. As we set forth in a previous letter, Genetics Journey identified close family members that you indicated you were unaware of. We have contacted those family members, who also took the Genetics Journey, and then have assented to releasing their names and place of residence to you.
    Though Genetics Journey makes every effort to ensure accuracy and precision in its testing, we do not warrant or guarantee the results in any way. You may wish to get additional testing to verify our results. Our testing has identified the following relatives:

Kyle Angetti of Orange, MA	uncle or cousin
Kevin Angetti of Orange, MA	uncle or cousin

Again, thank you for trusting us to help you on your Genetic Journey.

Very truly yours,

Jenna James
Family Liaison

Elizabeth Grace Adams
450 Millington Commons
New Salem, MA 01355

January 2, 2015
Dear Gretchen:

    Now that I have passed my eightieth birthday, I am making plans for when I will no longer be with you. I have placed my will and information on my investments in my safe deposit box at Third National Bank. My credit card information and plans for my funeral are in the safe in my room. The combination is the north group. Please use the money wisely but not too wisely. You were always too serious, and I'm afraid I often encouraged you in that.
    Know that I love you still and will even after death. You are my wonder child and do not ever forget it. I was raised from Yankee stock, and don't often show affection, but do not doubt that I wish all the best for you.
    I have kept a secret from you for decades. When you gave birth to Armand's child, at a very young age, I encouraged you to have the child adopted and to continue on with your swimming career. I still believe that was the best solution at the time, but I could not bear the thought of my grandchild growing up without my knowing how he was doing. Yes, you gave birth to a healthy baby boy, though you never saw him. I persuaded the Angettis, who were successful business people at the time, to take in the child and raise him as their own. The Angettis have had some tough times recently, but they

have always done well by the child. Kyle Angetti is your son and Kevin Angetti is your grandson.

Please forgive me for this deception all these years. I only wanted what was best for you and want to know that you are happy.

Love and affection,
Mom

CHAPTER THIRTY-THREE

Todd and I walked out of the house and into the car. He sat for a moment, his hands on the steering wheel, looking out the window.

"We need to go see Kyle Angetti. And Kevin," he said.

"Are we going to the state police?"

Todd shook his head. "We're not sure this is related to Grace's death. Or just sordid details from her past. I don't want to dig all this up if it's not necessary."

That was the small-town cop I loved. He knew people got embarrassed and didn't want their secrets revealed. "Let's go see the Angettis," I said.

Kyle Angetti was sweeping the yard. He stopped and leaned on the push broom as we approached. "Can't afford a janitor," he said. "Got to do the cleaning up myself."

If Betsy had picked the Angettis because of their prosperity, they had fallen down the economic ladder since the adoption. Kyle had done some illegal things, including selling marijuana, and had spent time in jail. Now, he couldn't afford a janitor and all four people working on cars were related to him. From the grease and dust covering everything, not many of them did any cleaning up.

"We just talked to Gretchen Connelly," said Todd.

"I know. She called." Kyle went back to sweeping the yard. "Said you might head over this way."

"Is there some place we can talk in private?" asked Todd.

"Not much privacy around here." Kyle looked around. "There's a picnic table out back. Nobody's due for a break for another half hour."

We made our way to the back where two redwood picnic tables sat, along with a small charcoal grill. We sat down.

"Gretchen said you knew about me." Kyle started in before we asked any questions. "I've known most of my life that I'm adopted. Didn't know about Gretchen and Armand being my parents until I was an adult."

Todd stared at Kyle. "And you didn't think to mention it when Grace was killed?"

"Didn't have anything to do with Grace. It's just part of who I am. I don't think about it much." Kyle took a pack of cigarettes out of his pocket and lit one. "I keep saying I'll quit." He blew out a stream of smoke. "But not today. What do you want to know?"

"Did you tell Grace she was your sister? Did you fight about it?" Todd asked.

"Hell, no." Kyle studied the end of his cigarette. "Grace came storming in here, a few weeks before she died, saying that she just found out. Told her I knew all along. She left."

I was sure there was more beyond that bare rendering. Did Grace threaten him? What could she threaten him with; he already knew. Was Grace angry at her mother and her grandmother? Did she go to confront Armand?

"Do you know where Grace went when she left here?" Todd was doing that cop thing, like he didn't care about the answer.

"Don't know. Just was glad that she was gone. And kind of glad that it wasn't a secret anymore."

Kevin came around the corner, talking as he came. "Hey, Dad, I need—" He stopped when he saw us. "Sorry to interrupt, but Allan needs to know the price of parts for the Subaru."

"He'll wait," Kyle said. "We're having a discussion here."

"Kevin, you're part of this discussion too," said Todd. "Why don't you sit down and join us?"

"They know that Gretchen and Armand are my biological parents," said Kyle.

A flicker of annoyance shot across Todd's face. Maybe he didn't want that piece of information out there just yet. He controlled his facial muscles and went on. "When did you find out, Kevin?"

Kevin didn't take a seat, and looked like he wanted to leave immediately. "Always knew Dad was adopted. He told me a few years ago about them."

"And you worked with Grace and never brought it up?" I asked. It seemed that they would have discussed their relationship at some point.

"Dad told me not to." That seemed to settle it for Kevin.

"Did either of you see Grace the day she died?" Todd continued with his questions.

"Not me," said Kyle. "I was here all day until someone came to tell us there'd been a murder."

"What about you Kevin? Did you see Grace that day?"

"Don't know." Kevin looked back over his shoulder to the place he came from. "Don't remember what I was doing that day."

"Was he working that day?" Todd asked. Neither Kevin nor Kyle said anything. "I can check the time records, if you can't remember."

"Don't keep time records," said Kyle. "It's all relatives. I pay them by the job." He stubbed out his cigarette in an ashtray that was already overflowing. "Kevin wasn't here when we heard the news. He had a doctor appointment that day. Check with the doctor."

"What doctor did you see that day?" Todd poised his pen over his notebook.

"Can't remember," said Kevin. He looked down at the table and tapped his fingers in a pattern from left to right. "I'll look it up and let you know."

"Something wrong with you?" asked Kyle. "You always see Dr. Matthews, ever since you were a baby. You seeing another doctor, 'cause something's wrong?"

"No," said Kevin. "Everything checked out fine." He looked up at Todd. "I'll get you the name when I get home tonight."

Another man, in coveralls and carrying a book, came around the corner. "Kyle, I got a customer on the line. I need to know about the estimate on the Subaru."

Kyle stood up. "I've got to deal with this." He looked at Kevin. "We'll talk about this later." He and the other man left.

Kevin stepped back from the table. "I got to get back to work too."

"Sit down." Todd was in full cop mode. I'm not a cop, but I didn't believe Kevin's story about a doctor either. Maybe he did have something to do with Grace's death.

Kevin sat down and pulled his chair up to the table. When Todd got in this way, everybody seemed to do what he told them. Kevin was no exception.

"Where were you on the day that Grace died?" Todd asked.

"I didn't see Grace that day," said Kevin. "What I was doing had nothing to do with her."

"I don't know that." Todd turned the page in his notebook and picked up his pen. "You tell me where you were, I write it down and check it out. If you were where you said, it's not a problem."

"It is a problem," said Kevin. "You can't tell my dad where I was."

"Were you doing something illegal?" I asked. "Is that what you don't want to talk about?"

Kevin blushed. I don't often see a man blush, but the red rash spread from his neck to his forehead. Maybe he wasn't doing something illegal, just something embarrassing. I couldn't imagine what would embarrass Kevin. Or maybe everything embarrassed him.

"I got an alibi." Kevin looked around. "But you got to promise not to tell Dad."

"I can't promise that," said Todd. "But I promise not to tell him unless it's absolutely necessary."

"That's not good enough. He'll kill me if he finds out." Kevin seemed to realize a few seconds too late what he said. "Not kill me, but make my life miserable."

"I can make your life miserable too," said Todd. "I can arrest you for murder." Todd stopped talking, a technique he often used. The next step was up to Kevin.

"Okay, okay." I saw Kevin look up and wrinkles appear on his forehead. It looked as if he were making a decision on the spot. "I was with my friend, Steve."

"Does Steve have a last name?" Todd tapped his pen on the pad.

"Everybody has a last name," said Kevin. He dropped his head to his hands, folded on the table. A few seconds passed before he looked up. "Steven Milford."

"What were you doing together?" asked Todd.

"We were, you know, together-together." Kevin put his head back down on the table.

I took Todd's notebook from him and wrote on the page "Steve Milford's prints were in the barn at SRVHS." Todd nodded. He remembered, of course he remembered.

"What's together-together?" Todd asked.

Kevin sat up straight in his chair, but he looked past Todd's right shoulder. "Steve is good to me. He buys me things and takes me places I've never been. Like the amusement park and the gardens at Tower Hill. We even went to the corn maze." Kevin's head tipped back and he stared at the sky. "I like Steve. A lot."

"Where were you and Steve when Grace died?" Todd continued with the questioning, despite Kevin's discomfort. I know he wanted information, but it was painful to watch.

"We were at my house. But nobody else was there that day. Just me and Steve."

"And why don't you want your father to know?"

"Because he's, you know, traditional. He don't think that boys should be together."

I saw Todd nod his head at the same time I realized what Kevin meant. He was trying to protect Steve. I had my doubts about whether Steve needed protection, but, if the story checked out, neither of them had killed Grace. How Kevin would deal with his father was an issue for another day.

"But Steve was at the historical society," said Todd. "His fingerprints were in the barn. The barn that nobody was supposed to be in."

"Yeah, that may have been a little bit illegal. Are you going to arrest me for that?" Kevin stopped after the question. When Todd did not answer, he started speaking again. "Steve didn't have a place to stay. I told him nobody was around in May, so he could stay in the barn. I let him into the bathroom to wash up and sometimes he came to my house to take a shower. But he didn't kill anybody. He was with me."

"Did you and Steve try to sell the stuff from the museum?" asked Todd.

"That was stupid," said Kevin. "Steve really needed money, so he took some things and said he could sell them on the internet, nobody would know."

"But the things were brought back to the museum," I said. "I think everything was returned."

"Yeah," said Kevin. "I know how important the stuff was to the museum. I told him to bring it back. But I didn't want him to get caught, so we put it in the barn. Just barely got it back before the locks were changed."

"You returned the items after the police were finished?" I asked.

"I knew you were going to change the locks," said Kevin. "It was our only chance. But I put everything back in the barn. Steve helped me when he saw how important it was to me."

Kevin looked around, as if seeking guidance in the sky. "It's all there. I checked. We didn't keep any of it." Kevin stood up. "Are you going to arrest me?"

"I'll check out the story and get back to you." Todd closed his notebook. "If everything is there, things will go easier for you."

Kevin left, dragging his feet and looking back over his shoulder.

CHAPTER THIRTY-FOUR

Todd and I walked out to the car. He pulled out his phone and reported our conversation to Trooper Gray. Judging from the sounds coming from the phone, she was not happy with what he did. But she did agree to check out Kevin's alibi. And she added that she would check the whereabouts of the other members of the family, including Kyle. Her voice had just returned to a normal level when Todd told her about the family connection between the Connellys and the Angettis. I don't know about him, but I was glad when that phone call ended.

"Looks like I'm in trouble with the state police," said Todd. "It's not as if I could've predicted where this day would go. At least I'm keeping them in the loop. That's more than they're doing for me."

I leaned back in the seat. Suddenly, I was exhausted and all my bones ached. Of course, the baby took this opportunity to start kicking.

"Looks like he's pretty active today," said Todd. "Do you want me to take you home?"

"I don't know what I want to do," I said. Though home and sleep did sound good. Then I remembered what happened to my car the last time I was here. "What about the ampersand?" I asked.

"Ampersand?" Todd was searching his memory. "That 'and' thing in the notes?"

"Yeah," I said. "The 'and' thing in the notes. Jesse was so proud of it, said it was his idea to have the ampersand. I haven't seen anybody else in this matter use it, have you?"

"No," said Todd. "And it's just fuzzy enough that we shouldn't turn it over to the state police until we know more." I didn't know whether he was trying to convince me or himself, but it sounded good to me. Suddenly, I didn't feel so tired.

"I'll go with you," I said. After all, it was my discovery and my idea.

"No," said Todd again. This was getting tiresome. "Armand has turned up in some strange situations and he's been keeping a secret. I think I should go talk to him alone."

He drove me home. We argued all the way, but he was adamant that I wasn't going with him. He finally used his best argument: I would be putting our child in danger. He was right. I wasn't just protecting myself anymore; I was also protecting my child. That was my responsibility. He did come into the house to make sure I had what I needed for the rest of the day. I also suspected that he wanted to make sure I was in the house before he left. But maybe I'm just overly suspicious. He got me a blanket and a cup of tea and left me on my computer, searching for parental support groups. Barney came over to join me. After he determined that I had no treats for him, he went to sleep.

After about thirty minutes, I was restless. And the baby was kicking again. I found Barney's leash and we went for a walk. My life wasn't so bad. I had a man who loved me and a dog who depended on me. I was ready to be a mother. I liked my job. It wasn't the life I'd imagined when I went away to school in Boston. I'd envisioned myself working in a university archive library, helping people do important research and finish their doctoral thesis. But I liked my more balanced life now, with time to raise my child.

A car pulled in my driveway as Barney and I arrived home. I slowed down, not trusting anyone at this point. Irene, the museum's administrator, got out of the car.

"How are you doing?" she asked. She took a couple of steps back when Barney went to sniff at her. "Is you dog friendly?"

"Yeah," I said. "Though he might lick you to death. What are you doing here?"

"Just wanted to see how you were. And I brought you some soup." She pulled a thermos out of the car. "It was the only thing I could keep down when I was pregnant."

We walked into the house. Barney behaved himself and went to lie on his dog bed. Irene sat at the kitchen table and I made tea.

"Do you want some soup now?" Irene asked.

I shook my head.

"What's wrong?" Irene sounded like she was interested in me, not just going through the formalities.

"It's confusing," I said. "I'm pregnant and I always thought that a child needs two parents who are committed to each other." I sat down at the table and put a mug of tea in front of each of us. "But Todd seems to have reservations. He even waited to tell his other children." I realized this conversation directly contradicted my earlier thoughts.

"He seems like a good man and people seem to like him as chief of police." Irene put sugar into her tea.

"Yeah," I said, "but some of the things that make him a good cop are a problem with us. He's suspicious of everyone and is leery of marriage because of his prior experience. And since I learned my baby may have learning difficulties, he's pulled further away."

My phone rang. Curtis Hapgood again. "I wonder who this person is. He's called several times." I showed the phone to Irene.

"He's the assistant director of the archival library at Massachusetts University," said Irene. "I asked him to give you a call."

"For what?" Massachusetts University had resources I only dreamed of. I couldn't imagine what they needed from me.

"About a job," said Irene. "They're looking for an archivist and I suggested you."

"A job? Me?"

"Why not you?" asked Irene. "Just to give you some options, other than a part-time job where funding is always an issue."

"But I like my job. It's only part-time, but it means that I can stay in New Salem with Todd." And it was the only job I could find after graduation. Of course, I'd learned a lot in the last four years.

"Is that what you want?" asked Irene. "This job could open up possibilities for you. Massachusetts University has onsite day care, you'd be making a lot more money, and you'd have more options for the future."

"But I'd have to commute from New Salem to Massachusetts University every day. That's forty minutes each way."

"Unless you moved closer. Lots of people do that," said Irene. "Think about it. And call him back."

I called Curtis Hapgood back. He seemed anxious to meet with me and I promised to send him my résumé and references. We set up an interview for the following week.

Irene and I finished our tea. She left and I realized she had given me options aside from staying with Todd, should I need them.

I looked around the house, to the dishes in the sink and the unfinished nursery. Neither task appealed to me. I'd started taking charge of my life and I wanted answers. I might not be able to solve Grace's murder, but I might be able to figure out who left the notes on my car. Armand was the major suspect. I needed to know what was going on. One phone call wouldn't hurt. The converted factory that housed Armand's Curiosities & Collectibles was in the center of town. I dialed the number for the main office.

"Armand's Curiosities and Collectibles. Jesse speaking."

"Hi, Jesse. This is Emma Wetherby. Is Todd Mitchell there?"

"No," said Jesse. "My dad went to meet him at the Orange police station. Said he had some questions for him. Do you know what that's about?"

Maybe Jesse knew something about Armand's business that I might use. Armand was out of the building, talking to Todd, and this might be my chance to see what Jesse knew.

"Are you alone in the building," I asked, "or is someone else watching the store?"

"I'm in charge." Jesse's voice rose slightly, as if insulted that I challenged his abilities. Not a great start. I could handle this.

"Great, Jesse, maybe you could help me." I tried to piece together a plausible story on the fly. "Todd and I are preparing for our new baby, and I wanted some vintage toys for the nursery. Do you have anything like that you could show me?"

"Of course, we have a whole selection of antique toys." I knew that from previous experience, but he went on. "I'm sure we have something that you could use."

"Great," I said. "I'll be there in thirty minutes."

CHAPTER THIRTY-FIVE

I'd based it all on the ampersand. What if I was wrong? What if I was accusing someone who was innocent? A kid who was innocent.

Breathe in. Breathe out. I can do this. I'm just asking questions. I pulled into the driveway of Armand's Curiosities & Collectibles, an old factory building right over the river. The fire station was across the bridge, on the other side. Maybe I should call the police; maybe I should've called them already. No, I was here, I needed to do this. Guess I was more nervous than I thought, as I almost hit a pile of wooden pallets when I pulled into the parking lot.

The door was open. Not a lot, just enough to let in a sliver of light. No truck in the driveway. Armand had already left for his appointment with Todd. I pulled open the door and walked in.

The light was directly over the entrance and it gave the only illumination to the gigantic warehouse. The wide planks on the floor, black from years of factory oil, had gaps between them. The brick walls exhibited exposed pipes and conduits. It all smelled like river water and machinery.

The windows over the river, ten feet high and with deep sills, all had wooden shutters over them, so only a weak streak of light came through. In here, you wouldn't know that the sun was high overhead. Stuff was piled everywhere. Glancing around, I saw copper tubing, car parts, neon signs, and wooden figures.

"Hello," I yelled. "Hello, is anybody here?" My voice echoed through the building. Nothing moved.

Steps ran up the left side of the room. They were steep and, at the bottom, was a yellow-and-black-striped sticker that said "Watch Your Step." It looked like it had been there since the factory days, as the ends were coming loose. I started up.

The second floor had the same huge windows overlooking the river, though these windows were uncovered and streaked with some white substance. Guess washing windows wasn't a priority for Armand. Here, the sunlight reflected off rows of shelves filled with dolls, toys, books, and household and cooking utensils. I shook my head at Armand's decision to have a cluttered first floor—a bad first impression—and an organized second floor.

I heard a noise; sounded like a shriek and a shudder. No doubt what that was: someone had opened a warped window on the third floor. I started up another, even steeper, set of stairs.

When I got to the top, I saw Jesse. He was sitting on the wide sill of a window overlooking the river. I could see him because the third floor was remarkably clear of clutter. Probably used as office space, as it contained two desks and some filing cabinets.

Jesse turned toward me. "Don't come any closer or I'll jump."

If he expected me to stop, he was mistaken. I took several steps closer to where he sat.

"I said don't come closer." Jesse shifted in the window. "I'll jump."

I went to the neighboring window and looked down. "Unlikely to kill you," I said. "Probably just get wet and covered with gunk from the river. Maybe break a leg."

"The dam's just down a ways. The current gets faster there." Jesse leaned out the window and looked down. "I miss her so much."

"I miss Grace too," I said.

"Not like me." Jesse banged his head against the window frame. "I wanted her to be my mom. I don't remember my real mom."

I didn't know what to say to that, so I said nothing.

"She got along so well with my dad," Jesse continued. "They both liked old stuff, they laughed together. My dad can tell by looking at something how old it is. But Grace knew what people liked, what would sell."

"Sounds like they made a good team."

"We were all a team. They were teaching me about the business, so I could take over some day. I thought it would be perfect if they got married. We would be a family. Grace just laughed at me. Said it wasn't going to happen." Jesse pointed to a box on the floor. "Those were the last things we bought together. I can't stand to take them out of the box or to look at them. I can't go through them. Maybe I'll just jump."

"Jesse, just give it some time. Maybe you'll feel different tomorrow." It sounded lame to me, even as I said it.

"How come you want to help me, after I sent you those letters?"

I'd come here to confront him, but didn't expect him to bring up the topic himself. "So you did write those notes to me."

"Yeah." He looked like a five-year-old caught in a lie. Complete with pouting lip. "I just wanted you to leave us alone."

"Then why send me the notes?" I asked. "You know that would get the cops involved."

"But I told you not to contact the cops. I just wanted to scare you."

Everyone knew I lived with the chief of police. But Jesse seemed to believe that I would do what the note said.

"Just like with Grace," Jesse continued. "She never did what I wanted her to do."

"Grace was trying to take care of you." I didn't know if that was true, but I needed to comfort the kid and get him out of that window.

"And then, and then..." Jesse wiped his nose on his sleeve.

I looked around for tissues. None in view. Of course not, this was a man's office; they didn't plan for people to cry. All right, I was hungry, I was having an inane conversation with an adolescent, and I was getting bitchy. I took a deep breath.

"And then what happened?" I asked.

Jesse swung his legs around, into the room, and looked directly at me. "Then she got that stupid DNA test. I gave it to her for her birthday, because she was so interested in her ancestors. They were having a sale."

It sounded like Jesse knew about his father's affair with Gretchen, Grace's mother. But I had to be sure. "What about the DNA test?"

Jesse didn't answer for several seconds. His words came out in a whisper. "Then she found out she had a half-brother: Kyle Angetti." Jesse slapped his hands on his knees. "And then she yelled at Dad for not telling her."

"Why did she yell at your father?" I was missing something here. This was the first I'd heard of a fight between Armand and Grace.

"Because I got a DNA test for my father too."

Jesse was shaking his head and slapping his hands on his knees. He looked like he couldn't sit still and yet he didn't move from the window.

"Why was that a problem?" I asked. I didn't know where this conversation was going, but it didn't seem to be anywhere positive.

"'Cause he was related to Kyle Angetti too," said Jesse. "Kyle is his son."

"And then what happened?" Not the most brilliant question, but I was at a loss.

"Then Dad explained that he had always thought of Grace as a daughter, though they weren't biologically related. And wasn't I glad I had a sister?" Jesse stopped talking, pulled a tissue out of his pocket, and blew his nose. "But I wanted a mother. I wanted Grace to be my mother." Tears rolled down his face and made his shirt collar wet.

I felt that I should comfort him, but he didn't seem like he wanted to be touched. He looked too miserable sitting there, hanging his head and looking down. The hell with it; I went up to him and put my arm around him. He pulled away, though there wasn't much space left on the sill.

"Leave me alone. I already told you that."

I stepped back. At a complete loss as to what to do next, I chose to do nothing. I still didn't have any answers about what Armand and Grace were fighting about, how Jesse was involved, or why he sent me the notes. "I'm going to the police station," I said.

"Why?" Jesse seemed genuinely confused, as if this was not a possibility he had considered.

"Because they need to know that Grace and Armand fought. They need to know about the family connections, though they may already have some idea." I stopped talking for a moment. "Your father is at the police station with the chief. We need to get out of here before he comes back," I said. "Let's go."

"Where?" Damn, this kid was stubborn.

"To the police station. To tell them what you just told me."

"I don't want to get arrested," said Jesse. "I don't want to go to jail."

"They're not going to arrest you," I said, "but they need to know that your dad was fighting with Grace. They'll need to investigate that."

"My dad didn't do anything," he said. "It was me." He looked down at the river.

"What did you do?"

"I killed Grace." He rubbed his eyes, though they were already red and swollen. "I didn't mean to. I just wanted to talk to her."

Jesse was almost six feet tall and he hauled around furniture with his father. He was strong enough to swing the metal seal and kill Grace, but I'd never considered him as a suspect. He seemed like a lost kid. "How did it happen?"

"I heard her and Dad arguing over the DNA test. I wanted to tell her it was okay, she could still be my mother." Jesse wiped his eyes on his sleeve. "We weren't really related, so she could still marry my dad. She said no."

"Why were you at the historical society? How did you get there?"

"I told her to meet me there. Told Dad I'd do the pickups that day. I just wanted to talk, but she kept saying she wasn't going to get married." He put his legs back up on the sill. "When I told her I needed a mother, she just laughed. Said that wasn't their relationship. It's a mess."

Before I could stop him, Jesse tumbled off the sill and into the river below. I ran to the window and watched him hit the water like a rag doll. He seemed to make no effort to swim, but just sank. I thought of jumping after him, but I didn't know what lurked beneath the murky waters. I turned and ran down the stairs, past the piles of toys and other junk, looking for something to help me.

I ran out the door and to the back of the building. A stack of pallets was in the center of the parking lot, and I grabbed one and pushed it into the river. It floated. My mind registered someone yelling from the opposite bank, in the direction of the fire station, and I hoped it was help on its way.

As soon as I went into the river and grabbed onto the floating pallet, the current swept me toward the dam. Assuming this was the direction Jesse was going in, I hung on with one hand and put my face into the river, scanning the muddy bottom. I tried not to think of the myriad of bacteria and other creepy things floating in the water. I saw a shock of hair just below me, reached out, and grabbed. Jesse popped up on my left side, gulping for air. I guess he'd just figured out what I already knew: drowning was a horrible way to die. He shook his head and reached out to me.

"Don't grab on to me. Grab on to the wood." I didn't want him to panic and drag us both under. I repeated the instructions.

He put one arm onto the pallet and grabbed underneath with the other. By this time, we had been swept by the current toward the opposite bank, but were still way too near the dam. I kicked with all my lifeguard training and dragged us toward the side. There were trees along the river and the running water had exposed the roots. I tried to grab for one of the roots, as Jesse pulled the pallet closer to his body and back into the current. We drifted past several more trees.

"Just hang on," I said. "Don't try to guide us." I realized that I was gasping for breath myself, but the urgency seemed to get through to Jesse. "Let me grab one of the roots."

"I don't want to die." Jesse reached for me.

"Then do what I say and we'll get out of here." I wished I was as confident as I sounded. Visions of us banging into the dam and being sucked under flashed through my mind. With a last, desperate grab, I hugged one of the tree branches. It dragged my side of the pallet out of the water, but Jesse held on.

I'm still not clear on what happened next. There were sirens, and ambulances, and people in the water. They dragged me and the pallet out of the river. Jesse, too, I guess, because I remember his yelling about not meaning to kill himself. He disappeared into an ambulance.

CHAPTER THIRTY-SIX

I woke up to pain in every part of my body. Even my teeth and hair hurt. The antiseptic smell and beeping machines could only mean I was in the hospital. I tried to raise my head, but the pain stopped me from looking around.

I must have made some sound, because a face hovered over me. "How are you feeling?"

It's a common question in the hospital, but it was still a stupid one. If I was feeling good, I wouldn't be here. My hands went to my abdomen. Still had a bump there, but no movement.

"Your baby seems to be doing fine," said the face above me. "I'm Amanda, your nursing assistant." She fiddled with the tubes on a metal pole. They probably went into my arm, but I wasn't moving my head to find out. "The baby's heartbeat is strong. He didn't seem to mind the dunking in the river."

My hands were scratched and red where I'd clung to the tree roots. I even noticed some slivers that hadn't been removed. I tried to tell Amanda, but my voice came out as a croak.

"Here, have some water and some ice chips." Amanda put her arm behind my back and lifted me up, to put a cup to my lips. There was a moment of pain, then the pleasure of the cold water in my mouth. I realized that I couldn't say more than a few words.

"Todd," I said.

"Yeah, that handsome cop of yours. I'll send him in." Amanda left with a little wave.

I finished the ice chips while I waited. Took a deep breath. Something seemed to be working, because I felt better.

Todd opened the door and strode into the room. "How are you feeling?" he said.

I didn't answer that question. "What happened?" Must be the ice and cold water were working, because he seemed to understand me.

"You and Jesse were fished from the river by the fire department," said Todd. "Jesse's under arrest and in another part of the hospital. You've been checked out and, other than cuts and bruises, you seem to be fine."

My hands went back to my abdomen.

"I almost lost both of you," said Todd. "You could've gone over the dam with the baby. It was a stupid thing to do."

I didn't much like the idea of being called stupid, but it hurt to talk. That seemed to be fine, because Todd continued on.

"Jesse is being held in a locked psych ward. He was anxious to confess, claimed he did the murder himself, his father didn't know anything about it." Todd pulled a chair over and sat down. "The whole thing's a mess."

"Why?" I asked. Even that was an effort.

"Jesse thought he, his father, and Grace were going to be a family. Yeah, it looks like both Grace and Armand had a bit of a grifter in them, though they never did anything illegal. They thought the items they bought would be cheaper with a story. A story that said they were a couple and really wanted authentic antiques in their new house. I guess Jesse heard the story enough times, he started to believe it. In some ways, he's not very mature."

"How do you know that?"

"While you and Jesse were in the river, I was talking to Armand about the missing items. He said that Grace wouldn't steal from the museum, that she thought it was part of her heritage. The history was important to Grace, so she wouldn't steal from the historical society. But she and Armand adjusted their story to suit the buyers, also, to get the best price for items."

I was right; the mystery did go back to the creation of the Quabbin Reservoir.

Suddenly, I was exhausted. The last thing I remember is Todd leaning over to give me a kiss.

CHAPTER THIRTY-SEVEN

They kept me overnight in the hospital. Early the next morning, Irene showed up with a bundle of wildflowers. I identified yarrow and lilies, with a large amount of greenery.

"I thought you were more of a wildflower person, rather than a greenhouse person." Irene pulled a vase from her purse, added water and the flowers. "They won't last as long, but I'll get you more later."

"Thanks," I said. "I love wildflowers. How did you know?"

"Just being around you. It's not hard to figure out." Irene sat in the only chair in the room. "Do you need a ride home?"

"No. Todd's coming later with some clothes that don't smell like river water."

"I talked to Curtis Hapgood," said Irene. With everything that had happened, I'd forgotten about my job interview. "He said that, if you can't make it next week, he'll reschedule the appointment. Or you can do it by Zoom. He really wants you to work with him."

"Thanks for arranging that," I said.

"I saw Kevin at the historical society today," Irene continued. "He's talking about moving out of his uncle's house and moving in with Steve. And Steve has a job at the local diner. Things are looking up for them." She moved the vase closer to me. "And your sister left a message for you, at the historical society. She said that she's in Georgia with her family and she thinks you need some time apart."

"Interesting that Hadley called work, not my home. Guess she didn't want to talk to me, just leave a message. She knows I'm not happy that she went back to Jim. She doesn't know he's no good for her."

Irene looked directly at me. "And what about Todd?"

"What about Todd?"

"Is he good for you?" Irene asked.

"That's not fair," I said. "Todd doesn't hurt me. You said he's a good man and a good cop."

"He is a good man," said Irene. "But is he the man for you? Does he meet your needs?"

I started to argue with Irene, but stopped myself. Todd hadn't committed to me or to the baby and he'd been pulling away lately. Maybe I needed to rethink this whole thing.

"What would you do if you were me?" I asked.

"I'm not you," said Irene. "You need to make this decision for yourself. But now, at least you have an opportunity for a job and a life of your own."

She left.

For the rest of the morning, all the talk on the ward was the transfer of the prisoner from the hospital to jail. I guess I was getting a better deal than Jesse. At my request, Todd showed up with sweatpants and a red maternity top. No way was I leaving the hospital in the scrubs they gave me, two sizes too big, even with my pregnant body. And I refused to put on a johnny, with the opening in the back. Amanda, the nursing assistant, helped me to get dressed. On the second day, my hands were even more red and stiff. By the time I was dressed to leave, I was already exhausted. Todd also brought a bouquet of red roses.

Per hospital protocol, we left with me in a wheelchair. Todd brought his pickup truck and I must have made some sound when I realized I'd have to get myself up and in the cab.

"Sorry, hon, it was this or the cruiser. Your car is still at the warehouse and they haven't released it yet."

Todd helped me into the truck and closed the door. He climbed in and started the truck.

"Is there anything you want to get on the way home? I picked up some food and your medications, but we can stop if you need anything else."

"I just want to get home."

Todd put the truck into gear and we left the parking lot. We sat in silence until we left town. We were going down Route 202 when the silence got to me. We passed the place where Hadley went off the road.

"Do you know what happened to Hadley and her kids?" I asked. "After she went back with her husband?"

"He picked up the whole family and they moved out of state," said Todd. "Georgia, I think. He said he didn't want to deal with this town anymore."

"That's what Irene told me," I said. "I worry about Hadley. And the kids. They're not safe."

"You can't save everybody," said Todd. "That's one of the first things you learn as a cop."

"As an archivist, I want to save everything," I said. It wasn't much of a joke, but Todd grinned. Time to ask the questions I really wanted answered. "Have you talked to Jesse since yesterday?"

"I can't talk to Jesse," said Todd. "I have a relationship with one of his victims."

"I'm one of his victims?" I asked. "Since when?"

Todd explained that, because Jesse had sent me threatening letters, I was considered a victim. Because I found Grace's body, he couldn't be involved in that investigation either. Something in his voice told me there was more to the story.

"But you have connections," I said. "So you know what's going on. Why did Jesse think Armand and Grace were going to get married? Was the stealing just a story? What will happen to Jesse now?"

"One at a time," said Todd. "Grace and Armand, as part of their presentation about the artifacts and their history, also presented as a couple. Guess this was part of the grift, to think that what was being sold was authentic and from the museum. They were so good at it, even Jesse was convinced."

"But what about Armand and Gretchen? And Betsy, and Gretchen's father?"

"You know a lot about that already. Betsy had Gretchen at thirteen and couldn't have any more children. She put all her time and energy into bringing up Gretchen. When she showed talent as a swimmer, and was in the running for the Olympics, Betsy worked three jobs to make sure she could attain her dream."

"I'm not sure it was ever Gretchen's dream," I said. "Seems more like it was what Betsy wanted."

"We all want what's best for our children," said Todd. "Betsy was just more aggressive about it."

I looked out the window. We were almost home. "Then Gretchen got pregnant."

Todd pulled into the driveway and turned off the car. "Yeah, and Betsy didn't want her to give up on her dreams. So she arranged for the child to be adopted by a couple in town: the Angettis." Todd explained that, given her history, Betsy wanted to see her grandchild grow up, even if it was in another family.

"But why didn't she tell Armand and Gretchen?" I asked. "If she wanted a relationship with her grandchild, why couldn't they have a relationship too?"

"Different times," said Todd. "Birth mothers were told to forget about their adopted children."

"How can you forget about a child?"

"You can't," said Todd. "That's why Armand is sticking by Jesse. Don't know what's going to happen to him, but Armand got him a decent lawyer."

Todd got out of the truck, came around, and helped me down. He put his arm around me and asked if I could make it on my own. I said yes, but he kept his arm in place. We started across the lawn.

CHAPTER THIRTY-EIGHT

Of course, Troopers Bachelor and Gray showed up at the house and I had to tell my story again. And again. The local newspaper called me a hero. Todd called me foolish for jumping into the dirty river when I was pregnant. All this was running through my head when Gray and Bachelor arrived. I made us tea and the three of us sat down at the table. They had requested that Todd not be present for this interview.

"Tell us again what happened."

So I went through my story again. "I guess both of us were right. It was a combination of history and current drama."

"Yeah," said Gray. "Jesse said he was trying to reason with Grace. He had built up a fantasy in his mind. He and Grace and Armand would be a family and make a lot of money by using Grace's knowledge of the museum to get people to sell to them. Grace resisted. I guess she really was invested in the museum, but not Armand."

"She cared a lot about what we were doing there. Too bad Jesse didn't understand her motives. But why were she and Jesse at the museum earlier on the day that she was killed?"

"According to Jesse, that wasn't planned. They met at the museum, as usual, and they saw someone in the barn. When they went to investigate, that person ran away. Then they started talking about the museum, the store, and Jesse made a statement about how great it would be when Armand and Grace married. Grace seemed to make fun of his plans, and the argument escalated from there." Gray finished her cup of tea.

"Who did they see that day? Was it the Milford kid?" I asked.

"That's the most reasonable explanation," said Bachelor. "He was living in the barn. Arranged by Kevin Angetti, who's now been cleared of all charges. Unless the museum wants to prosecute him for trespassing."

"He didn't do any harm," I said. "Of course, it's not up to me. I'll discuss it with the board. Also what we need to do about Kevin, who clearly broke the rules. Not that any of their actions would get them jail time."

"And Jesse is only seventeen years old and it seems to be a homicide without premeditation," said Gray. "How long he gets will depend on whether the judge thinks he can be rehabilitated and whether he shows remorse."

"When we were talking, before he went into the river, he seemed to be a confused kid who didn't realize what he was doing. Even jumping into the river, I don't think he meant to die."

"There is that," said Gray. And our conversation ended.

CHAPTER THIRTY-NINE

"You need to pack."

It was three days until Brian and Dierdre's wedding, and I still hadn't bought a dress or started packing. Todd sat on the bed, reminding me of that fact.

"Do you want to sit down?" I looked up and Todd was patting the bed next to him.

"No, I'm fine." But I wasn't. My son was sitting directly on my bladder and the only dress that still fit me pulled across my breasts. I did need to go shopping.

"I'm so tired," I said. "But I did get some good news today."

"What's that?" Todd was not as focused as usual. In fact, he was scattered and didn't seem to be paying attention to me.

"I got offered a job. A full-time job as an archivist."

Todd looked at me. "I thought that Swift River couldn't afford a full-time position."

"It can't," I said. "The position is with Massachusetts University." I sat down next to him. "It comes with onsite child care."

"You're going to put our baby in day care?" he asked. "Without asking me?"

I took a deep breath. "I need to live my own life," I said. "You don't want the same things that I do."

"That's not true." Todd pulled a small blue box out of his pocket. "I got you a ring and everything." He opened the box. A marquis-cut diamond glittered in the light. Proving, once again, he didn't listen to me.

"I know it's a diamond," he said, "but the jeweler said that this is a traditional engagement ring, and I know you like traditional."

He believed the jeweler, who he had just met, over me. About what I would like. I sat on the bed next to him.

"Do you want me to go down on one knee?" he asked.

"No," I said. "I'm sure I don't. This isn't what I want."

"I thought you wanted an engagement ring. So I got you one." He moved the box closer to me.

"When did you plan on getting married?" I asked.

"Let's just get engaged for now," he said. "We can talk about a wedding day later. After this weekend, when Brian and Dierdre get married. Everyone will be so happy that you have a ring."

"No, they won't." I closed the box and gave it back to him. "Because I'm not going to the wedding this weekend."

"Not go to the wedding? Everyone is expecting you to be there. I even told Dierdre that we were getting engaged. She's happy for us."

"I've made other plans for this weekend. I got a signing bonus; that will be a deposit on my own apartment, closer to the university. And I've made arrangements to stay on campus in student housing for the next month, until the students return."

"You're not staying with me? What will I do?"

"Anything you want to. But I'm moving out."

The baby gave a kick of approval.

About the Swift River Valley Historical Society

The Swift River Valley Historical Society in New Salem, Massachusetts, seeks to preserve the memories of the four towns—Dana, Enfield, Greenwich, and Prescott—drowned beneath the waters of the Quabbin Reservoir. Boston needed drinking water so, in 1938, the four towns were disincorporated and the Swift River Valley was flooded. The historical society consists of the Whitaker-Clary house, still without indoor plumbing or central heat; the Peirce carriage shed, home of the 1929 Model A Dana firetruck; and the Prescott church, moved from its original site to the historical society and updated to be handicapped accessible and heated.

The Swift River Historical Society is open from June to September. More information can be obtained at:

www.swiftrivermuseum.org

Acknowledgments

I am so glad that you read the acknowledgments because this is where I get to thank all the people who help me in life and in writing. I am grateful to the Wednesday Morning Writers and to the Bodies in the Library, two writing groups that have made me much better at what I do. The Wednesday Morning Writers remind me that I am not alone in this endeavor and the Bodies in the Library provide ongoing, valuable critiques of my work. Special thanks to the many people who read large portions or all of my manuscript. In reverse alphabetical order, thanks to Elizabeth Tennessee, Robin Shtulman, Gwenn Meredith, Julie Logwood, Diane Kane, Mary Ann Faughnan, and Kathy Chencharik.

This is my third novel with Stillwater River Publications and I can't say enough good things about them.

And thank you to my family, who support me in so many ways, even when I make them crazy. My mother, Marilyn McIntosh, continuously asks me about the next book. My son Tony, and his wife, Tina, have given me inspirational grandchildren in Alex, Abbi, and Brent. This book is dedicated to the newest additions to our family, my nephews, Mac and Billy, both named in honor of my late father, William McIntosh.

About the Author

J. A. McIntosh, a recovering attorney, still lives in the small Massachusetts town where she was born. She writes the Meredith, Massachusetts series about imperfect people seeking justice. Her latest novel, *Swift River Secrets*, is her first novel with historical elements. She is the president of the Swift River Valley Historical Society. She also belongs to Sisters in Crime, Mystery Writers of America, and the Straw Dog Writers Guild.

REQUEST

Reviews are important to an author. If you enjoyed this novel, please take a few minutes to leave a review on Amazon, on Goodreads, or wherever you get your books.

Reviews show booksellers that people are reading and encourages them to spend money and resources to produce more books.

Made in the USA
Middletown, DE
04 November 2024